SURVIVAL FICTION LIBRARY
BOOK TWO
LOW PROFILE

Creative Texts Publishers
PO Box 50, Barto, PA 19504
www.creativetexts.com

Creative Texts Publishers products are available at special discounts for bulk purchase for sale promotions, premiums., fund-raising, and educational needs.

Survival Fiction Library: Book Two- Low Profile
by Jerry D. Young
Published by Creative Texts Publishers
PO Box 50
Barto, PA 19504

Copyright 2008-2017 by Jerry D. Young
All rights reserved
Cover photo modified and used by license.
Credit: Rich Moffitt via Foter.com/ CC BY

This book or parts thereof may not be reproduced in any form, stored in a retrieval system, or transmitted in any form by any means—electronic, mechanical, photocopy, recording, or otherwise—without prior written permission of the publisher, except as provided by United States of America copyright law.

The following is a work of fiction. Any resemblance to actual names, persons, businesses, and incidents is strictly coincidental. Locations are used only in the general sense and do not represent the real place in actuality.

Createspace Edition
ISBN: 978-1542807029

SURVIVAL FICTION LIBRARY

BOOK 2: Low Profile
By

JERRY D. YOUNG

CHAPTER ONE

Bobby Jones called to his next-door neighbor, "Hey! John! Come take a look see."

John Havingsworth controlled his frown. Bobby was always wanting to show him something, usually to do with either his guns or his Jeep.

"Look at these tires! Had to raise the lift another two inches!" Bobby beamed with pride. "Won't be no stopping me this time. You'll go, won't you? I need a cheering section."

John knew that if he didn't take a close look at the Jeep's new tires, Bobby would pester him until he did. He feigned interest as he took a long, careful look at the huge, aggressive tread tires. "Big," John finally said. "Some lug pattern,"

"Yeah! I won't have no trouble on Crunch Hill with these! Come on, you going or not?"

John didn't really want to, but when Bobby got in a foul mood he would start to get a little scary. "Sure, Bobby, what time?"

"Six sharp, Saturday morning. Uh... You probably should bring a pair of leather gloves. I might need you to help me with the winch."

With a nod John said, "Okay, Bobby. Just like last time?"

"Nah! Be a bunch better now, with the better tires and higher lift. You shouldn't have to get down in the mud this time."

Though he was careful not to say it out loud, John thought "Yeah, Right." What he actually did say, however, was "Okay Bobby, I'll be ready. Six AM Saturday morning."

To John, it looked like Bobby was about to bring something else up, so he hurriedly said, "Gotta go, boss wants me to come in early for a project."

"Hey, man! When you going to grow a spine? Tell that jerk you work regular hours. You got lots of things you could be doing besides spending all that time at work. It's not like you get overtime the way I do. You should look into getting into my line of work. All the commercial carriers are looking for delivery people."

"My job is not that bad," John replied carefully. In actuality, John had a good job that he liked. He was on salary and didn't get overtime, but the company was generous with a bonus program. John regularly got bonuses. In fact, the bonuses were what funded his emergency preparations. His preps were simple, but extensive.

"Well," Bobby said, "I guess it suits you. I'd find it booorrrriiiinnnggg."

"I'll see you Saturday morning," John said. He walked over to his driveway and started to get into his Subaru Outback wagon. It was no rock climber, but it did what John wanted it to do, which was to get him back and forth in all but the most extreme weather. John began to smile when he thought of the vehicle he had parked in a self-storage facility in the small town near Adam's farm.

If he hadn't known Adam Markum since grade school, and shared a few interests with him, John would never have been able to afford the rent on the 12 x 30 storage room housing the highly customized 1993 Chevy one-ton pickup truck and a portion of John's preps. Bobby would flip if he knew about it. The truck, like the Subaru, was no rock climber, but it did boast some pretty good get-around features. One of these days John might just have to show it to Bobby, for meanness if nothing else.

SUBURU OUTBACK

    Saturday rolled around and John went over to Bobby's house to go with him to the Mud and Rock challenge meet. He wound up waiting a full fifteen minutes before Bobby came out of the front door of his house. There was no apology, or recognition of the fact that it was Bobby's fault that they were running late, just Bobby's, "Hurry up! Don't want to be late."

    At least the Jeep was already loaded on the transport trailer. John guided Bobby as Bobby backed his Dodge Ram pickup toward the trailer. It took several tries, as Bobby over-steered the truck on one attempt after another, but finally, the trailer was attached. John threw his leather teardrop shoulder bag into the back of the Ram and climbed into the passenger seat.

    "Wait till you see what I do to this baby, after I'm finished with Sally Sue back there," Bobby boasted, patting the dash of the Ram.

Bobby had told John recently how much he was paying for the Dodge. It was taking half of what Bobby made every month to make the payments. John had to admit that Bobby had a pretty low mortgage payment, but with what Bobby was spending on the Jeep, John didn't see how Bobby was keeping his head above the water financially.

John put it out of his mind and enjoyed the weather on the trip to the site of the competition. At least, he enjoyed it as much as he could, considering Bobby's very aggressive driving style. They were honked at several times, and John lost track of how many times they got the bird. Of course, Bobby shot the bird right back, and was none too easy on the horn when someone was ahead of him in the passing lane and wouldn't speed up or slow down to let him go around.

Regardless, they made it in one piece. Bobby went to register, leaving John behind to un-strap the Sally Sue and lower the ramps on the trailer. John waited for Bobby to come back to unload the Jeep. He would have been fine to unload it himself, but Bobby wouldn't let anyone else drive it.

The event went about the way John expected it to go. Bobby got further in each event than he had in the past, but he still came in well out of the money....and of course, John was wet, muddy, and bloody. He'd had to handle the winch line in the mud crawl and on the rock climb. John knew that if he wasn't getting some valuable experience, he'd never go with Bobby. It sure wouldn't be worth it, otherwise. Bobby had even forgotten to bring a lunch and had to share John's.

The following weekend went about the same. Only this time it was gun-shooting time rather than off-roading time. Bobby was late on his insurance payment for the Ram, so they took John's Subaru to the range. John helped Bobby carry his bags of goodies to the firing line and then went back to the Subaru for his own shooting bag and gun case. They had the small range to themselves.

Each of Bobby's long arms was in an individual ballistic nylon carrying case. He already had his Romanian SKS out and was loading it when John made it back. "Don't forget your shooting glasses and ear protection," John called over to Bobby.

"Oh, Yeah." Bobby fished in his pistol bag, brought out the safety items, and put them on.

John barely had his own Peltor Pro-Tac II ear protection on when Bobby cut loose with the SKS. He fired the entire ten rounds as fast as he could. All told, Bobby fired a hundred rounds of the 7.62mm x 39mm and then set the SKS aside. He'd been firing at the one-hundred-yard gong. It sounded more often than not, but the hits were erratic.

John was just getting ready to fire his old lever action Savage 99A .308 Winchester. He loaded six rounds in the magazine and closed the action, chambering the first round. He sighted through the Bushnell 2.5-10x40 scope, set at 2.5 magnification, and began aiming at the one-hundred-yard gong. When he was settled, he fired all six rounds, slowly resighting for a second between each round. The gong sounded six times.

He dialed up the magnification and fired at the six-hundred-yard gong. Of the six shots he fired, four sounded the gong. The scope was mounted with an old Pachymar Lo-Swing scope mount John had found online. He flipped the release and let the scope lay alongside the receiver. He fired another six rounds at one hundred yards using the ghost ring rear receiver sight, again hitting the gong each time.

When he tried the six-hundred-yard gong with iron sights he made only two hits out of the six shots he fired. John swung the scope back into place and put the

Savage back in its place in the two-gun hard case he carried his long arms in.

"That's it?" Bobby asked, now holding a Bushmaster Carbon AR clone in M-4 configuration. He slid a thirty-round magazine into place and turned back to the firing line.

"Yeah," John said. "Just want to keep my eye in."

Bobby shook his head and began to dump the thirty rounds of 5.56mm x 45mm NATO ammunition down range. John heard the occasional clang, but couldn't tell which gong Bobby was actually aiming at.

John had his Stoeger 12-gauge coach gun out, ready to load, when Bobby had emptied four more thirty-round magazines. Again, there were plenty of gong hits, but they were very erratic. Bobby put the Bushmaster aside and took out his Remington 870 pump 12-gauge.

"You on safe there, Bobby?" John asked after Bobby had loaded the 870 and set it down.

"Uh…" he pushed the cross-bolt safety button on and then worked the action to unload each of the shells that he'd just loaded into it and said, "Yeah." Bobby had at least learned to follow John's safety rules. John had said he wouldn't shoot with him any more if he didn't.

They went to put up paper targets on the fifty-yard target supports.

When they were back behind the firing line, Bobby picked up the 870. He had added a collapsible stock with pistol grip and an extended magazine. John waited with the Stoeger broken open, two shells in the chamber, with two more held between the fingers of his left hand while Bobby reloaded the 870.

John let Bobby fire all seven rounds down range before he closed the action of the coach gun, fired first one barrel and then the other. With a quick motion, he opened the action, the two empty shells flying over his right shoulder. He slipped the other two shells into the chambers, closed the action, and fired twice more.

They walked down to the fifty-yard line, pinning up pistol targets at seven, twenty-five, and fifty yards.

Before changing the fifty yard targets, John was about to admit that Bobby's target was peppered with about the same number of pellet holes as John's, when Bobby gleefully pointed it out. John didn't mention that Bobby had fired seven buckshot rounds to John's two. There were also two large holes in the paper of John's target. The two slugs John had fired were about three inches apart, one inside the six ring, and the second inside the five ring.

Next they both opened up their pistol bags. John took out his father's old Colt 1911A1 that had been combat modified and fine-tuned back in the eighties. His father had never shot it much after he'd bought it.

Bobby took out three handguns from his pistol bag and put them on the shooting bench. He took a long, 33-round 9mm magazine and slid it into the butt of the Glock Model 17. As usual, Bobby emptied the magazine as quickly as he could. He slipped in another and did the same thing.

John, on the other hand, inserted a ten-round magazine into the 1911A1 and proceeded to fire rapid, aimed fire, at his target. He did a magazine change and continued to fire. Bobby was loading a Smith & Wesson 629 .44 Magnum with an 8⅜" barrel.

Bobby fired the first six rounds much more slowly than he had with the Glock. He loaded six more rounds and fired them also, before putting the gun aside. John had noticed in their few times at the range together that Bobby always shot the .44 Magnum, but only a couple of cylinders worth.

Next, Bobby picked up the third gun he'd set out. It was a little Raven .25 ACP semi-automatic. "Don't know why I shoot this," Bobby said. "It's just my throw down gun. You know. Just in case." He grinned and then fired the Raven.

It went off, but didn't cycle completely. Bobby racked the slide and fired again. That time it worked and Bobby pulled the trigger four more times, the Raven firing each time. Bobby picked up the live round that he'd ejected, opened and held the slide back to put the round into the chamber. He released the slide and fired the pistol. "Good enough," he said, dropping the empty weapon back in the pistol case.

The two walked out to check the pistol targets. Bobby admired the many holes he had put into the seven-yard target while John checked his target. John was a little disappointed that only two of the four rounds he'd fired at the seven-yard target were in the X-ring. The other two were in the nine-ring. Still, it wasn't his best shooting.

The rounds in the twenty-five-yard target could be covered by the palm of his hand, with one flyer near the edge of the target paper. Bobby didn't say much about his twenty-five, or the fifty-yard targets. John was pleased with his fifty yard results. All eight rounds were in the chest area of the target. Not extremely tight, but acceptable for John's wants.

They gathered up the paper targets and went back to the shooting bench. After they'd recased the weapons, the two went back to the Subaru to stow them.

LOW PROFILE

"I gotta get a carry permit!" Bobby said suddenly as John drove them back home. "I don't know why they won't give me one; that little scuffle was nothing. Think I'll get a lawyer and see what he can do." Bobby lapsed into a brooding silence.

It didn't bother John. Bobby's silence, brooding or otherwise, was a welcome relief. If Bobby hadn't talked about moving recently, John thought he just might have been making plans to move himself...and he hoped Bobby didn't get that carry permit. It was a scary thought.

John managed to avoid Bobby for the next two weeks, but all good things come to an end. Bobby showed up on John's doorstep one Monday evening. "Hey man! You got to help me out! I'm almost out of gas and I got to get to work. Christmas is the busy season and I can rack up a lot of overtime if I can get there. Boss said he'd fire me the next time I missed if I wasn't dying. Also, you got to loan me a few bucks for gas. I get paid Friday. I'll pay you back then."

Avoiding sighing openly, John pulled out his wallet and gave Bobby a twenty.

"Uh... John Boy... I'm kinda short on food at the moment, too. How about another twenty for some eats?"

Reluctantly, John handed Bobby another twenty-dollar bill.

"Thanks man! I'll pay you back when I can." With that he was off the stoop and running toward the idling Ram.

"But you said..." John's slight protestation faded away. "I'll never see that forty again," he mumbled to himself.

They pulled into their driveways at the same time that evening. John almost said something when he saw Bobby take out a small bag of groceries from the truck, along with a twenty-four pack of beer. Instead, he shook his head and drove into the two-car garage.

"I can't believe I'm going to move just because of him," John muttered, opening the yellow pages to find a real estate agent as soon as he entered the house. Suddenly he slammed closed the yellow pages book. "No, doggone it! I am not going to move because of him!"

In a sour mood, John went downstairs to the basement. One section was finished while another, smaller section, contained the utilities. The third section, the largest of the three, John used for storage. Of course, it was also a PF 1000 fallout shelter. The ceiling was pretty low to accommodate the shielding above it, but John could stand upright. He took out a #10 can of Mountain House freeze-dried seafood chowder. He marked it off the inventory. He scanned the inventory sheets. Time to reorder a few things. He'd do that this weekend.

Working with his preps always cheered John up. He made a serving of the seafood chowder and a small dish of fresh coleslaw for his supper.

John woke up the next morning to three inches of snow on the ground. He had a hot breakfast of oatmeal and then went out to clear the driveway. He saw Bobby get into the Ram. Bobby had cleared a small section of his windshield, but that was all. John was opening the garage door when Bobby backed out onto the snow-covered street.

Bobby finally saw John just as John was about to enter the garage. "Hey John! You want a lift? That little car of yours will never make it in this!"

"That's okay," John said with a wave. "I'll chance it. It does pretty good in snow."

"Your life, partner. Don't say I didn't offer." Bobby goosed the Ram and the rear of the truck slid over two feet.

John heard Bobby curse. Bobby must have put the truck in four-wheel-drive mode, because the next time he goosed it, the truck stayed straight and Bobby roared off.

John took his time and cleared the driveway with his snow shovel, and then his section of sidewalk. He started to put the shovel away, but then sighed and walked over to Bobby's driveway and cleaned both it, and his sidewalk.

After putting the snow shovel away, John got in the Subaru and headed for work. He took it slow and easy and made it fine.

John couldn't believe it when Bobby came over two days later. "Hey man! Need to talk to you! I need to pick up some food. That blizzard is supposed to hit tonight."

"Don't you have something put away? A three-day supply, at least? Geez!"

"Aw! You know me! I just get what I need when I need it."

John, getting more fed up by the day, let his annoyance show, even as he was taking out his wallet again. "What would you do if it was the end of the world? Nothing in the shops?" He regretted it as soon as he said it.

"You think about stuff like that?" Bobby asked, taking the twenty John handed to him.

John suddenly saw a glint in Bobby's eyes that he didn't like.

"Hey man!" Bobby said, "If it's the end of the world... I got guns and ammunition. I'll get what I need, don't worry."

"Okay, Bobby," John said, feeling sick. He tried to lighten up the conversation and get it away from being prepared. "Don't spend it all in one place."

"Probably have to. It's only a twenty." Bobby looked at John expectantly.

John handed over another twenty silently.

"Thanks man! I knew you'd come through, and don't worry, it's going to be a few days, but I'll get this back to you." Bobby went off at a trot to his truck.

John silently cursed himself for letting Bobby get to him like that. He'd always made it a point to keep his preparations a secret. He used the 'gray man' approach, keeping a very low profile. Bobby might not think anything about it right now, but if anything ever happened…

CHAPTER TWO

John carried a box of #10 cans of freeze-dried food into the house, and then went back to the Subaru for the three sacks of regular groceries he'd bought on the way from picking up the LTS (Long Term Storage) food from the storage room. He was always careful to only bring one preparedness item to the house at a time. The box brought him back up to where he wanted to be in terms of LTS food at the house.

Although he never really thought of himself as having enough preparations, he did have things set up at the house according to his long-range plans. He pretty much had the hardware he wanted over all, except for a real retreat.

He had space reserved in the shelter at Adam's farm, with his own supplies stored. It was a reciprocal deal. Adam had some supplies stored in John's shelter in the basement and he and his family were welcome in a disaster. Both men had additional supplies and equipment in the storage room that Adam rented to John at a discount.

Adam had relatives in Kansas to whom they could go if the situation was such that staying local was not an option. Adam had also told John he would be welcome to come along, but John wasn't so sure. From what Adam had said about his brother, a stranger showing up on his doorstep might not be welcome, despite what Adam claimed.

As an alternative, John did have a small piece of land in Missouri. There was a small cave on it that John considered a last-ditch refuge. Besides some hardware, John kept several years of basic food stored in the cave. There was a year round spring a quarter mile away from the entrance to the cave where John could get water to replace what he had stored as it was used.

John hoped never to have to use any of the preparations, except to rotate them, but Mother Nature being the way she is and Father Time being the relentless soul he is, and human beings being what they are, it was pretty much inevitable that he would have to use them.

The first real test of his preparations was due to Tulsa being a major transportation hub, with several railroads, major highways, and the Tulsa Port of Catoosa on the McClellan-Kerr Arkansas River Navigation System. Transportation hubs invariably had hazardous materials going through them and Tulsa was no exception.

Among the hazardous material were chlorine, propane, diesel, and gasoline, sometimes all on one train. Combine that situation with domestic terrorists and you have the makings of a disaster.

John heard the crash and the first explosion a few minutes after he got home. He was only a few blocks from the point on the tracks where the terrorists had chosen to sabotage. Not knowing specifically what the trouble might be, but knowing what passed over the tracks five blocks away, John decided his best course of action would be evacuation...but first some protection. He opened the hall closet and pulled out the respirator bag hanging next to a white Tychem SL hazmat hooded and footed protective coveralls. After pulling the Millennium CBRN respirator out of the bag, he put it on and snugged it into place. He reached up and got a

CBRN canister and screwed it into place on the mask. He took a deep breath. He could breathe.

John both felt and heard the next explosion. It prompted him to hurry with the protective coveralls. He put it on over his suit and snugged the hood down around the rim of the respirator and tied it in place. Still working with haste, but holding the panic down, John slipped on a pair of BATA overboots. He did a good turn and a half of duct tape around the top of each boot, sealing it to the coveralls. Next he put on Nitrile gloves and taped them.

He was hearing sirens now, getting closer and closer. He then heard another explosion, this one louder than the two before. After grabbing his personal BOB from the floor of the closet, John ran into the garage and hit the garage door opener on the run. He was in the Subaru and had it started in moments. As he backed out of the garage, he saw people running down the street. He also saw Bobby standing in his yard, beside the Ram.

Bobby waved at John and ran over to the Subaru. John was rolling down the passenger window and called to Bobby, the ESP II voicemitter of the respirator amplifying his voice slightly. "Hey man! You got to get out of here!"

"What's going on? Why are you wearing that? Where is it?"

John didn't want to take any more time, and when a wisp of faint green mist drifted toward Bobby, Bobby quickly opened the door of the Subaru and dived in, closing the window and door at the same time. "Go! Go! Go! Go!"

Being careful not to hit any of the running people, John got the Subaru onto the street. They could see the green mist thickening. The wind was directly toward them, and coming from behind. As soon as he could take a street perpendicular to the wind direction, he took it.

"Are you crazy, man!" Bobby screamed, as others continued to run from the mist. "Hey! You got another mask?" He coughed a little when John drove through a tendril of the mist and some of it came in the car.

"Come on, man! Give me a mask!" Bobby was reaching for John's respirator when John had to slam on the brakes to avoid a car pulling out onto the street. Bobby's right side hit the dash, and he slumped back in the seat, the impact having knocked the air out of his lungs. He struggled to breathe, and John was sure Bobby was trying to get up enough wind to try and take John's respirator.

About the time that Bobby, with a crazed look in his eyes, began to struggle up and try for the respirator again, they came to a police line and John slowed. The police officer motioned for John to roll down his window. Bobby was protesting, but John did it anyway.

The officer took a moment to look at John. "You a First Responder?"

John shook his head. "Private citizen. And this is my... friend. How far should we go?"

"You should be okay in this direction now, but I'd say to keep going for a while. People on foot are going to be congregating no further than they have to go."

John nodded and pulled past the police cruiser. Bobby had heard everything and seemed to be losing his panic. When John found a spot where he could pull over, he did so and unfastened the hood of the protective coveralls. He then removed the respirator. John could tell Bobby wanted to reach for it when John tossed it onto the rear seat of the Subaru.

"It's a relief to get out of that thing," John quickly said. "Guess I didn't need it, but I don't like to take chances." He looked over at Bobby then. "How you feeling? You got a whiff of whatever it was. Chlorine gas, I think."

"Poison gas?" Bobby began to cough.

"I'd better take you to the hospital," John said.

That seemed to satisfy Bobby. He quit coughing.

A nurse took a quick look at Bobby when John and Bobby walked into the lobby. "Over there. We'll look at you in a bit." She looked at John then. "Hadn't you better go after someone else?"

"I'm not Emergency Services. Just a citizen."

"Oh." She frowned and added, "Well, stay out of the way."

After fifteen minutes or so, Bobby began to get annoyed that the doctors and nurses were working on other people as they came in. They were obviously in much worse condition than Bobby, but that didn't seem to matter to him.

"I'm going to sue the city!" Bobby said, coming to sit down beside John after he'd gone to try to get one of the nurses to look at him. John noticed Bobby was only coughing when he was trying to get the attention of one of the medical personnel. John felt shame, both for Bobby, and for himself, for aiding and abetting the situation.

They were watching the coverage of the disaster on one of the Tulsa stations. From the reports, they learned that a mixed freight train composed mostly of tank cars had derailed on a slight up grade. A gasoline tanker had exploded, possibly with help from a bomb of some kind. The burning liquid fuel was running down the grade and it caught several more cars on fire, or caused them to overheat. At least one of the propane tankers had BLEVE'd and that had ruptured two chlorine tanks. (BLEVE – Boiling Liquid Expanding Vapor Explosion)

John decided, when one of the interns looked at Bobby and told him to get plenty of fresh air (and if symptoms got worse, to come back in), that the intern just wanted Bobby out of the area. John could understand why.

Apparently upset because the intern couldn't find anything wrong with him, Bobby was still muttering about suing the city and the hospital as they walked out to the Subaru. "Where do you want me to drop you, Bobby? We aren't going to get home for a few days."

"Geez! I don't know!" Bobby fell silent, and John was hoping he was thinking of some place he could stay. After a long silence, Bobby finally asked, "What are you going to do?"

It was a question John didn't want to hear, much less answer, but it was there, voiced, and he had to respond. "Get a motel room, I guess. I've got enough stuff to tide me over until I can get back home."

"Hotel? Man, I don't have enough for a hotel! I got… like twenty bucks!"

"What about a credit card? Don't you have one you can put a room and some food on?"

"All of them are maxed! I don't get paid till Friday and this is only Tuesday!"

"They'll probably be a shelter set up. Let's…"

Angrily, Bobby cut John off. "I ain't staying in no stinking shelter! I'm a man, not some little wimp that's got to go crawling to some shelter run by more wimps!"

"I don't know what to tell you," John said cautiously.

"Well, what about I stay with you? We're buddies, aren't we?"

John was disappointed in himself when he gave in. "Yeah. Sure. Okay. Come on, let's go." All the way to the motel John berated himself. He should have just said he was going to the shelter, and then left at his leisure.

LOW PROFILE

He wasn't about to share a room with Bobby, so he booked two rooms. He got a few strange looks, undoubtedly due to the protective gear he was wearing. He stripped it off when he got to the room. Flipping on the television, he watched the coverage of the train wreck.

John decided he was lucky he got the hotel rooms when he did. The evacuation of the area was on going, with a larger area now being evacuated. There were several more tank cars not yet involved, but could be if the fire was not contained.

It wasn't long before Bobby knocked on John's door. "You ready to get something to eat?" Bobby asked when John opened the door.

"I'm not really hungry. You go ahead. I'll get something later."

Bobby frowned. "Aw! Come on man! You know I don't have the money to eat on! You were going to stake me until I got paid."

"Sure," John said, carefully keeping his voice neutral. He definitely needed to do something about his 'friendship' with Bobby.

"You know," Bobby said as they entered a nearby restaurant, "I'm going to have to get me one of those suits and masks." He looked over at John and asked, "You have an extra you can loan me until I get one of my own?"

"Sorry, Bobby," John said evenly as they were taken to a table. "I don't have one I can loan you. I got mine on clearance online."

"Oh. Okay. It's just going to be awhile."

John was quiet during the meal. Fortunately, Bobby got off the topic of getting anything else from John, and went to expounding on what he was going to do to Sally Sue next. John followed along with half an ear, nodding or commenting when necessary. Finally, the meal was ended and John paid with one of his credit cards.

"Let's go see what is going on," Bobby said as they left the restaurant.

"We'd just be in the way. I just want to go back to the motel and rest up. I'll watch the coverage on TV and go to bed early. I have to be in to work early again tomorrow."

"Okay, lazybones. Let me have the keys to your windup toy, and I'll go get you a personal report."

"Bobby, I can't do that. You'll have to get a taxi or something."

"Why not? You know I'm a good driver."

"I just can't, Bobby. If you go down there they could very easily run you in for interference and impound my car."

"Some friend you are!" Bobby went to his room in a huff.

John didn't care. He was getting really tired of Bobby taking advantage of him. Of course, John let it happen, and he knew it. "It's my own cotton picking fault," he muttered as he turned on the TV again to watch the news.

He didn't watch long. The authorities had things under control. John went out to the Subaru and brought in his BOB, and the Subaru BOB. He'd planned to eat out of them, since he had three days of food in the personal BOB, and a week in the Subaru BOB, but Bobby had changed that.

After undressing, John took a shower. He got the toiletries ditty out of the Subaru BOB and brushed his teeth. He crawled into the bed naked. He called the front desk and asked for a 5:00 AM wake up call.

John groaned and rolled out of bed the next morning when the automated wakeup call came. Using the items in the toiletries ditty, he shaved and combed his hair. He had a change of clothes in the Subaru BOB, but they weren't really suitable for work. The underwear was, however, and he put on a fresh pair of boxers.

NATO GAS MASK

He shook out and brushed the suit he'd worn the day before and put it on as he watched the morning news. The story had made the national news. The worst disaster Tulsa had ever experienced, and it was confirmed that the derailment and first explosion had been an act of domestic terrorism. A group calling itself 'Americans For Safer Society' had claimed responsibility.

He felt a bit bad about leaving Bobby stranded at the motel, but didn't think about it for long. He decided to keep the food in the BOB's in reserve and stopped for a fast food breakfast before he went in to work.

The derailment was all the talk at work and John wasn't the only one at work affected. Two more employees called in saying they wouldn't be in due to it. He'd come in early just to avoid Bobby, but it was well he did. With the other two employees out, he had almost a triple load of work to do. Besides coming early, he wound up working late. He stopped and ate on the way to the motel, not really caring at the moment how it would affect Bobby's plans.

Bobby was upset when John pulled into the parking lot of the motel. "Man! Where you been? You left me stranded this morning!"

"We had two people out today. I had to go in early and stay late. I'm beat. I'm going to my room and get ready for bed."

"What about me? I'm starving! All I had today was that crummy Continental Breakfast the motel does."

"Didn't you get some lunch while you were working?"

"Working? How was I supposed to get to work? You ran off and I didn't have any way to get there."

"A cab would only have been a couple of dollars," John replied. He was tired and getting angry. "You said you had, what, twenty bucks?"

"Well, I had a few beers last night after you went to bed. No harm in that. I sure wasn't driving anywhere. Had to walk down the street. It's a lousy bar."

John sighed and took out his wallet. "Here's a twenty." He waved vaguely at the street. "There's fast food places close. If you walked to the bar, you can walk to one of them. I'll take you in to work in the morning. Hopefully they'll let us go back to our houses tomorrow evening."

He turned away, and went into his room, not waiting for Bobby's outraged response. John closed and locked the door in Bobby's face. He heard Bobby cursing, but couldn't make out the actual words.

John waited until Bobby had left and went out to bring in the BOB's again. From that point the evening was the same as the last. John turned in early.

He got up early again, shaved and combed his hair, and got dressed in the clothing from the BOB. It was a Friday and they had Casual Friday at work. John almost always wore a suit anyway, but decided this was as good a Friday as any to go in casual. He put the BOB's back in the Subaru and waited for Bobby.

John was fidgeting by the time Bobby put in an appearance. John called him over and when Bobby saw him, he laughed and asked, "Who are you supposed to be? Great White Hunter?" John was wearing a pair of khaki work pants and a khaki work shirt.

"Funny," John said as Bobby entered the Subaru. John headed for an IHOP for their breakfast. Bobby took his own sweet time over breakfast, and John called his office on his cellular telephone to let them know he was running late.

Bobby finally finished and they went back out to the Subaru. Both were silent, and John was thankful that Bobby was engrossed in the sports section of the paper that he'd asked John to get for him at the IHOP.

Without a word of thanks, Bobby got out of the Subaru at the carrier's offices. He leaned down and said through the open door, "Be here at 5:00." Bobby closed the door without waiting for John to answer. Fuming, John headed for work.

He was waiting, as Bobby had asked, at 5:00 PM that evening. It was a little after 5:30 PM when Bobby walked over to the Subaru. "I thought you said 5:00," John said when Bobby settled himself in the passenger seat.

"I did. Don't get off until 5:30, but I didn't want to have to wait."

John was amazed, but Bobby didn't seem to give what he'd done a second thought. On top of that, Bobby wanted to eat at Red Lobster, and he wanted a lobster for dinner. "Just got a craving, you know?" he told John after he'd put in the order.

John had just sat there, his mouth hanging open. He didn't say much during the meal. Bobby was flirting with the waitress, anyway.

"Where do you bank, Bobby?" John asked when they were once again in the Subaru. "I'll take you by so you can deposit your check."

"Wells Fargo, but I deposited it while I was on my run."

When they got back to the motel, John headed for the motel office.

"Bobby," he said, "Don't forget to pay for the room in the morning. I'm checking out then, too. If I can't get back into the house tomorrow, I'm going to stay with some friends."

"They shouldn't mind another one, should they?" Bobby quickly said.

"They don't have room. I'll be a real imposition, I couldn't ask them to put up two."

"Oh, too bad," Bobby replied. "This has worked out okay, me and you, working together. Even if you did stiff me yesterday."

Fortunately, the residents that had been evacuated were able to return to their homes beginning at noon the next day. There was still clean up to do, but the hazardous materials had all been pumped into tank trucks and removed.

John had gone into the office, just for something to do and heard the news on the TV in the break room. He finished off what he was doing and headed for home.

Bobby was already at his, working on Sally Sue as if nothing had happened.

After going inside and opening all the windows and doors to let the house air out, John went over to Bobby's. "Hey Bobby," he said. Bobby had his head under the hood of the Jeep.

"Hey, John. What's up? Good to be home, huh?"

"I'll say. About that money you owe me…"

Before John could continue, Bobby's head appeared from under the hood of the Jeep. "Yeah. That. Hey, man. It's going to be a bit before I can give that back to you. I missed a day's work and things are going to be tight for a while."

"I see," John said. And he did see…the parts boxes of a snorkel engine air intake kit. Brand new. Afraid to say anything else, John said "See you later," and walked calmly back to his house.

He considered it a defeat, but John checked the phone book and called the real estate agent he'd found previously. He was putting the house on the market. He'd start looking the next day for another place.

There were several open houses going on in the city. The market was down and there were some bargains to be had, but that also meant that John's current place probably wouldn't bring what it would have two years before. John looked at several places around Tulsa. He found one new subdivision going in that he liked. It was a new walled and gated community going in on the edge of the city.

It only had the two display homes built at the moment. He didn't particularly like either of them, but there was a large corner lot at the rear of the complex that had caught his eye. The market being down was to John's advantage when he started negotiating for the lot. He made it clear that the purchase of the lot was dependent on being allowed to put in a two-story

Quadraplex, with a basement. He would live in the basement and rent out the four above-ground units.

The owners didn't like it, but after three hours of consultation with all the partners, behind closed doors, the representative came back out to the waiting room of the offices and told John that the other partners had agreed. A stipulation was that the owners had the right to approve or bar any potential renters. The second stipulation was that the design had to blend with the tone of the complex. John would have to have the plans approved by the complex owners.

John wasn't fussy about the exterior design. As long as they let him build the basement the way he wanted.

John took that next Monday off to meet with his real estate agent. He came out to John's house to take pictures and put up the agency's 'For Sale' sign.

"With the railroad situation the other day fresh in peoples' minds, this could be a hard sale," Hubert Garcia told John.

"I'm not much of a negotiator," John told Hubert. "Price it high, and let potential buyers know there is a full-fledged fall… er… tornado shelter in the basement."

"Well," Hubert replied, "That will certainly make a difference to some buyers. I'm not so sure starting really high and then lowering price will work. It might backfire on you. Sometimes when a seller shows a willingness to drop the price, a buyer will take advantage of it and get the price even lower than what a good price would have been."

"I'll chance it." John shook Hubert's hand and said, "I'll be in tomorrow after work to sign the papers."

As soon as Hubert left, John went into the house and began working on the plans. Using the Quadraplex in the old HUD publication HUD-180-S as a starting point, John drew up a set of basic plans. Feeling a bit guilty about having the whole basement area as his residence and shelter, he kept the design features in the drawings in HUD-180-S that made the kitchen and utility room in each dwelling unit an emergency shelter with access to a bathroom.

With the basic dimensions for the foot print of the Quadraplex, John drew out the floor plan of the basement. He was smiling when he went out to the Subaru with the drawings. The owners of the development had been adamant about using one of their approved builders. John had looked over some of their example books while waiting for the decision. The designs of one specific builder had caught his eye. That's where he was taking the drawings to be reviewed and a set of working drawings made.

John was back at work on Tuesday, feeling better than he had in a long time. Even when he got home and Bobby walked over, John couldn't stop smiling.

"You're selling? Why?"

John had his story ready. "Thinking about retirement. I'm building a Quadraplex for rental. I'll live in one unit and rent out the rest. It's part of my retirement plan. With just four units, I don't fall under the same rules a large apartment complex does. Though it takes a big lot, it's not nearly as much property as four individual lots. The design takes full advantage of the lot, leaving large amounts of shared open property for all the residents. The overall cost of the quad is significantly less than the same square footage in four separate houses. I think it is one of the best investments there is, as long as it is being built with rental in mind. Durability and ease of maintenance. And that's how I'm having them built."

"Oh." Bobby looked a bit shell shocked at John's enthusiastic explanation. "Well... Good for you, I guess..."

"I need to get inside," John said. "I'm expecting a call."

"Sure... I'll see you later." Bobby walked off, looking dejected.

John almost felt sorry for him, but suddenly remembered how much money Bobby owed him and the circumstances under which it was owed.

It was a month before John got the first interested buyer for his house. It was a very low-ball offer, and John turned it down. It was about the same time the architect called and said the plans were ready. John picked them up after work and studied them that night. He had to admit, the elevation drawings matched the style of architecture of the display homes very, very well.

There were several notations on the basement drawings. John smiled. The architect hadn't questioned the why of the room layout of the basement, but commented it wasn't very effective use of the space.

That was fine with John. He planned on making a few on-site changes when it came to pouring the basement footings, floor, and walls.

John submitted the plans to the developers the following day, and got the approval for building a week later. Another week and the contractor broke ground. John spent every spare minute at the building site. Staying out of the way, mostly, but letting his presence be known so, when the time came, he could affect the changes he wanted.

It wasn't as difficult as he thought it might be. There were already many uncommon elements in the original building plans. The few changes that John instituted on site weren't questioned. He did have another, separate, contractor do a few things on the lot on two different weekends, in addition to the work the primary contractor was doing.

When the twelve-inch ceiling slab was poured, it was covered over with five feet of earth, which brought the monolithic pour for the floor of the quad two feet above grade. John didn't hang around as much during the construction of the quad itself. There were only a couple of details pertaining to the basement that were involved in the construction of the quad, and once added to the drawings, John was sure that they would be incorporated without any problems.

Knowing it wouldn't be too much longer that he would need to put up with Bobby on a regular basis, John didn't mind so much going with him to his Jeep events. Bobby even seemed a bit more mellow. Mellow for Bobby, at least.

John continued to check on the progress of the construction of the quad. He also began to equip the basement, but only during weekends when no one was around, and he could get a load from the old house to the basement under the quad.

He bought a few items specifically for the basement, however, and paid extra for weekend delivery to minimize witnesses. By the time the quad was finished and ready for occupancy, John had already moved in, lock, stock, barrel, and preps. Bobby didn't even give him a house warming present.

John began to breathe easy. He was even better prepared for disasters, human made or natural, then he had been before the move. Even better, all four units of the quad were rented within a month. The only problem was that his old house hadn't sold, so he decided to rent it out, too, until it did sell.

The rents from the quad were paying for the entire structure, including the basement. The rent from the house was gravy, and it went directly into preps.

Though he was pleased with the new preps, he was beginning to worry about the fact that he might very well need them. Things were really beginning to heat up politically in several spots around the globe, all at the same time. Also, the effects of global warming were becoming more obvious with the wild weather extremes being experienced around the world.

North Korea was threatening nuclear war with South Korea and the US.

Venezuela was rumored to have obtained nuclear weapons from North Korea or Iran, or both. They offered aid and assistance to Mexico to take the Aztlán territory from the US.

The leader of Iran announced that Iran was now a nuclear power and gave the UN three years to disenfranchise Israel, or else.

Rumors were rife that there was soon to be a political change in Saudi Arabia. A change not favorable to the US and her allies.

Brazil also joined the nuclear club, announcing a small nuclear arsenal, to be used in the case of threats of invasion.

The general population of Russia was showing great unrest with their current leadership. Crackdowns on dissent activities were beginning to take place by the government. The several crime syndicates that had developed after capitalism had come to Russia and were campaigning to keep democracy. There were reports that pitched battles between the gangsters and Communist sympathizers were taking place in several major cities.

The former Soviet republics had suddenly fallen silent.

China was conducting military training exercises along most of its borders and had announced she would be test firing several missiles over the course of the exercises.

Africa was in turmoil. More and more internecine, small scale wars were taking place.

Precious metals prices were climbing daily, as were all types of fuel prices.

One of the hottest summers on record in Europe hadn't helped things. People in the corn belt in the US had been losing crops due to drought conditions. Now they were suffering an overabundance of rain. There was flooding all across the Midwest. As November rolled around, a series of storms developing in the Northwest Pacific, all headed for Southwest Canada and the Western US.

The Pacific Rim was experiencing unprecedented volcanic and earthquake activity.

The inflation rate suddenly began rising, as the Fed poured money into the system to try to reduce and control the foreign debt problem, particularly that with China.

The UN was pressing the United States to take the lead in disarmament, not only of strategic and tactical weapons, but also civilian ownership of small arms, claiming that if the world's strongest power did so, other countries would follow suit.

The current administration in the United States was showing strong support for the UN call for disarmament. No less than six bills were on the floors of the Senate and the House to restrict civilian ownership of firearms, from a revived Assault Weapons Ban to a complete ban of all weapons, except for military and police.

Prices for all weapons, hi-cap magazines, and ammunition jumped sky-high. John was comfortable with his collection of weapons and accessories, and his supply of ammunition. He'd been on a buying program for a long time for arms, ammunition, and accessories, just like he had been on the buying program for gold.

John stopped those programs and began accumulating cash. He used three banks, all independent of one another, to handle his banking needs. At each bank, he had a checking account and a savings account.

He kept his balances in each under the FDIC insurance maximum. If any one of the banks had trouble, he still had funds in the others. Since there had once been a Federally mandated 'Bank Holiday', there could be one again. John began to draw down the balances of each account slowly. Just as he had with the banks, he stashed the cash in several different locations, for safety.

Adam Markum had large fuel tanks on the farm and John paid to have them filled so they would have a sure supply if fuel became hard to get. Adam would keep them topped off, as long as fuel remained available.

John also went in with Adam to purchase both biodiesel production equipment and supplies, and a set of alcohol production stills. The alcohol would stretch their gasoline supply by mixing it with the gasoline to produce E85 fuel.

John didn't know what else he could do to increase his level of preparedness. What he did do was put a television in his office, tuned to Fox News Channel to monitor the world situation. He also picked up a couple more Oregon Scientific NOAA NWS SAME alert radios. One for his office and one for the Subaru. If anything major happened he would know it as early as it was possible.

It seemed, however, that the old adage was true. If you are prepared for something, that something seldom happens. That was the way it was with John's preps. All the situations seemed to be calming down. Except the inflation rate. It continued to rise, a bit more slowly, but it was still going up.

John got another big bonus for his work and with gold and silver down somewhat from their highs, began the purchasing program again. He let one of his checking accounts grow slightly to cover the increased costs of everything, particularly food. Weather losses, fuel prices, and inflation were bringing the cost of food up slowly, but steadily.

There was nothing more to do, except wait for the other shoe to drop.

CHAPTER THREE

Drop it did, and it wasn't one of the things that had been bothering John. It was a problem that had fallen off the front pages. Avian Influenza. It was never clear where it got a foothold. It *was* clear that it spread from the Dallas/Fort Worth International Airport after a blizzard had closed the airport for two days just before Christmas.

Two weeks into the New Year, cases of human transmitted Avian Flu began to show up in ever increasing numbers all around the US and in several cities around the world. Adam's wife June was a nurse, and both her parents were doctors and preppers. On June's advice, John began taking a series of Tamiflu as a precautionary measure. It was one of many medications that he had stockpiled thanks to Arthur and Hillary Buchanan, June's parents.

The US essentially shut down. It wasn't martial law, but it was close. Everyone not in a critical industry was instructed to stay home, isolated, until the disease ran out of new bodies to infect. There were heavy losses in the medical profession, despite extreme sanitation measures.

John had no problem sitting out the first wave of the illness. The company shut down for three weeks, but advanced the employees a month's wages to carry them through. John cashed the check and added it to his cash reserves.

LOW PROFILE

He spent the three weeks in the basement shelter, watching the news for local and national information and listening to shortwave broadcasts for international news of the event. He also monitored the HF shortwave bands for information not semi-controlled by the government the way commercial broadcast news was.

Once he thought of Bobby, whom he hadn't seen in months. John quickly put the thought out of his head. Bobby was a big boy. He could fend for himself.

John worried a bit that the natural disaster of the flu might encourage adventurism by some aggressive countries, but nothing happened other than the loss of life all around the world.

Despite the early outbreak in the US, the country lost fewer people to the disease than many other countries, due to relatively good medical care. There were sixty-million deaths with another sixty-million hospitalized patients, recovering slowly.

Worldwide, the losses were higher in many places, upward of thirty-five percent dead and an additional twenty-percent hospitalized. Some nations with little medical infrastructure suffered much higher losses. Countries like Sweden and Switzerland had lower losses, due to their medical care. Australia had heavy losses in the cities, but many of the isolated small towns and independent ranches had very low loss rates.

John lost two of the four renters in his quadraplex. Disinfecting living and working spaces was a new, booming, business. He had the two units disinfected and was able to rent them again. With the inflation, rental rates had gone up, but with more availability and less demand, the rates dropped. John broke out about even, the rates on his quad units going back to what they were when he first rented them out.

Adam's extended family came through with flying colors. None had come down with the disease.

The pandemic created a mixed bag of effects. Due to the great loss of human life, many items were in surplus and prices for those items fell. Other items, because of labor intensive production, were scarce, with attendant higher prices. There did seem to be a trend. Necessities went up, luxuries went down.

Food was one of the necessities that went up. Adam was able to finance, at good rates, additional land for farming, and he added two greenhouses to the four that he already operated.

Fuel continued to go up as well. Adam hired two additional hands and set up the biodiesel and alcohol production units to start making fuel. Half of the additional land he had acquired would go to producing fuel crops. He put in two additional irrigation wells and pumps.

Two of the things that dropped in cost, despite the still pending legislation to ban them, were firearms and ammunition. Of the sixty-million dead in America, a significant number had been gun owners. All types of firearms came onto the market, and at very low prices.

John hit a small bonanza in finding the families of three different preparedness oriented men that had died during the pandemic. The families were looking to sell the preps, except for food, that the men had accumulated over the years.

John offered above the going rate to buy the entire lot of items in each case and took home several good acquisitions for his armory. He doubled his ammunition stocks. The firearms and ammunition he didn't want he held, expecting prices to jump again. Many other items that the men had, he sold and used the proceeds to buy more gold and silver coins.

After asking some leading questions, John also got maps from two of the families. They were maps of the men's caches. One of them had accompanying lists of the cache contents. The third man either didn't have caches, or had not put down their location on hard copy form.

John took a couple of days off and went looking for the caches. Both men had good descriptions with map coordinates and landmarks. Both also had global positioning satellite coordinates. The caches were easy to find. John left them as they were.

It bothered him a bit to acquire the items the way he was. Those men had labored for years to build up their preps. He was getting them for dimes on the dollar. But the families would have sold them in any case.

Much to John's surprise, gold and silver were coming down sharply in price. It seemed much of the second and third world peoples that had put away gold for emergencies, had turned it loose to get them through the tough days of the pandemic.

Taking advantage of that situation didn't bother John at all. He began buying all he could as the rates continued to drop, but the situation didn't last long. People were still people and nature was still nature. Neither were stable for very long.

The pandemic was the trigger for the return of Communism to Russia and the former Soviet Republics. The new Communist government began to solicit many of the former countries that had been in the USSR sphere of influence to rejoin them voluntarily. What would happen if they didn't was left hanging.

China began to close its borders again.

Suddenly the number of illegal border crossings along the US/Mexico fell dramatically. Some said it was because of the fence now going up, but that project had barely started. There were even a discernable number of illegals returning to Mexico and the Central American countries from the US.

The I-10 War broke out on a Sunday, with Mexico and Venezuela declaring war on the United States, with the announced intention of Mexico reclaiming the historical Aztlán territories of the Southwest US. Mexico submitted an appeal for the United Nations to support them in their endeavor to declare the historic Aztlán territories a part of Mexico.

Los Angeles was taken without an official shot being fired by a small army that had entered the US as illegal aliens over several years. That is not to say there wasn't fighting. Despite the gun laws of California, many gun owners began an immediate guerrilla action against the attacking force. Racial and religious prejudices on both sides resulted in numerous atrocities.

As Los Angeles was being taken over, Houston met a similar fate, with an in-place army augmented with Mexican troops off loaded from Chinese controlled ships. Houston was cut off, but there was no real attempt to enter the city in force.

Additional Mexican troops closed all border crossings and poured combatants northward, supported by troops from Venezuela. The largest group headed up I-25. US forces were slow to respond, although locals, as they had in Los Angeles, began fighting on their own, with heavy losses. There was much more air cover for the attack than had ever been expected. Reports began to come in that many of the planes were flown by Chinese looking pilots.

Congress was called to immediate session and the President, with approval of the Congress, declared war on Mexico and Venezuela. The President also warned China to get out of the conflict if they were in it.

The Mexican and Venezuelan armies hit the I-10 at several points and began to spread out on a front from Los Angeles to Houston. By Monday noon, the US military was retaliating. But Venezuela announced that if the US didn't step back and allow the takeover, the battle would go nuclear.

The President reined in the Armed Forces, insisting on a holding action along the I-10. They were not to cross the interstate under any circumstances. The situation would be evaluated and a decision would be forthcoming.

John watched the news coverage with amazement. It was inconceivable to him that the President was hesitating. John wasn't alone in his amazement. By Wednesday millions of Americans were protesting the lack of response of the US government. State after state had groups of armed citizens preparing to head for the border, with blood in their eyes.

When that became obvious, the President declared martial law, instituted curfews, and restricted travel to Federal Government approved reasons. There weren't many reasons for travel listed.

All the while Mexico was consolidating its positions south of I-10. It was allowing refugees to move north out of the invasion area, but they were allowed to leave only with the clothes on their backs. All other possessions were being confiscated.

All states' National Guard units were Federalized. Those states that had internal State Militias began to fortify their borders. Even northern states not likely to come under attack.

The President never said what she would have done to break the stalemate. Then one day Venezuela, apparently acting on impulse and without consultation with Mexico, launched three missiles from Venezuela northward.

Though the Air Force tried, they were unable to counter the missiles. Venezuela proved that it had not been kidding when they had announced the possession of nuclear weapons. Seattle, Omaha, and Chicago were hit with one-megaton nuclear weapons. Massive evacuations were begun around and downwind of the three cities.

The President didn't waver any more. Nuclear tipped cruise missiles were launched at Caracas, Venezuela and Mexico City, Mexico. US Forces were allowed to push the invading armies back into Mexico, though the ground forces were ordered to stop at the border. To the surprise of the members of the Joint Chiefs of Staff, they were ordered to eliminate the Mexican and Venezuelan Air Forces and to seize the Venezuelan oil fields.

Another big surprise was the orders to escort all known Chinese shipping out of US territorial waters. An embargo was imposed on Chinese shipping to the US. All products from China would have to be on non-Chinese ships. Many, convinced of China's duplicity in the I-10 War, wanted much more aggressive measures.

The presidents of Venezuela and Mexico were both killed by sniper fire a few days after the attacks within the borders of their countries. Venezuela and Mexico both surrendered unconditionally two days later.

It took several weeks to ferret out the leaders of the Aztlán Movement in and around Los Angeles and their army. Many small battles continued to occur during the process.

Though it was illegal, Hispanic heritage people all over the US were being driven from their homes and sent back to Mexico by locals. Only those that looked or sounded Hispanic that could show long term American citizenship were allowed to stay in many places.

The camps that weren't there opened up and took in the refugees from the targeted cities that had no other place to go, but many people relocated themselves.

Three weeks after the nuclear attack on the American cities, people were allowed to begin to return to their homes in the fallout affected areas. It was a staged return, as the radiation levels fell closer and closer to the targets. There were multitudes of occurrences of looting in the affected areas, despite martial law and travel restrictions having been emplaced early in the war. There were also many cases of radiation sickness of the looters that had stayed to loot and hadn't evacuated.

Quite a few people had refused to evacuate for reasons other than looting and received fatal doses of radiation. The number of cases of radiation sickness that didn't turn out to be immediately fatal numbered in the millions. The US health care system, already decimated by the Avian Flu, was overwhelmed again by the cases of radiation sickness.

The UN condemned the US for its use of nuclear weapons, even though it was in retaliation to those used against it. More calls for unilateral disarmament were voiced. Though those calls for strategic and tactical weapons were ignored, the US administration again called for total civilian disarmament.

Both sides cited the use of personal weapons during the war and its aftermath as arguments for and against private ownership of firearms. It was a controversy that wasn't going to go away this time.

Despite the recent war and the efforts of gun owners across the country, another gun ban went into effect. It wasn't nearly the law that anti-gunners wanted, but then again, it did restrict availability of some arms and as importantly, ammunition.

Full auto weapons were still covered by the old law. Bolt action, lever action, and break-open action shoulder arms need were taxed yearly at $25.00 if they had magazine capacities of ten rounds or less. If they had more than ten round magazine capacity, a $50.00 yearly tax applied.

Break open action handguns, single action, and double action revolvers, again with a limit of ten round capacity, were taxed yearly at $100.00 each. If they had over ten round capacity the tax was $200.00 each, per year.

Shoulder arms and handguns of .50 caliber or larger, no matter what type of action, were restricted to special license holders, at $1,000.00 per year for the license and $1,000.00 per year per weapon.

Semi-auto firearms with fixed magazines of more than ten rounds were taxed at $200.00 per year. Semi-auto firearms with removable magazines were taxed at $500.00 per year. Magazines over ten rounds had a purchase tax of $100.00, but were not taxed on a yearly basis.

All weapons did have to be re-registered each year and the tax paid.

A special purchase tax was also placed on the purchase of ammunition. No more than fifty rounds of any caliber ammunition could be purchased at one time, and there was a purchase tax of $25.00 dollars per transaction, no matter what quantity was purchased. Multiple calibers could be purchased at one time, but no more than three.

Rim-fire ammunition was in a separate class. It could only be purchased one 500 round 'brick', or the equivalent, at a time, and there was a $50.00 tax on the sale.

Firearm sales were limited to no more than one per month, six per year. Ammunition was limited to 1,000 rounds per caliber per year center fire, 5,000 rounds rim-fire.

Amazingly, private sales were not banned or taxed, though the new owner was supposed to register the firearm within ten days of the purchase and pay that year's tax on the firearm. Pre-1900 cartridge firearms lost their exemptions. All cartridge arms fell under the new laws. Non-cartridge firearms were still exempt.

With the high taxes on the arms, magazines, and ammunition, and the tough penalties for non-compliance, hundreds of thousands of firearms came onto the market. The actual price of most weapons dropped like rocks, even as the cost of owning them skyrocketed. The BATFE was quadrupled in size and tasked with actively enforcing the new laws. Existing registration records were used by one division to begin collecting taxes on weapons already registered. Another division went after current sales to ensure registration and tax collection.

The war didn't affect John much. He was able to continue to work, and when food deliveries were delayed due to the war and the travel restrictions that also applied to commercial trucks, John simply used a bit more of his LTS (Long Term Storage) food in a regular rotation.

He put in orders to replace what extra he was using, but was put on a long back order list. There were thousands of new preppers now due to the recent events. All the prep companies were receiving record numbers of orders. That included shelter manufacturers. The various internet prep and survival forums too were getting enormous numbers of hits every day as people looked to lock the barn door after the horse was gone.

John, like many others, took advantage of the reduced prices of firearms and greatly added to his collection. He was very careful to screen any and all offers, to make sure he wouldn't get caught in a sting. He passed up quite a few offers due to that fact, but he picked up quite a few firearms, and ammunition with most of them.

His Savage 99, Stoeger Coach Gun, and Colt 1911A1 were registered and he paid the taxes up front as soon as the law took effect. He bought two additional guns, from individuals, for his Cowboy Collection, and registered and paid the yearly tax on them. A Marlin 1895 Cowboy lever action .45-70 and a Ruger New Blackhawk .45 ACP/.45 Colt convertible. They, like the Savage, Stoeger, and Colt, were somewhat politically correct.

John also sold a couple of unregistered weapons, to get bills of sale. Of the weapons he'd bought over the last couple of years were two high tax weapons that he didn't particularly care for. He didn't mind losing them to get on the record as getting rid of that type of weapon. Both were AR-15 clones that had been somewhat abused. He let six magazines go with the weapons. They too, were in less than perfect condition.

All his other weapons were unregistered, un-papered, and well hidden. When the BATFE showed up, twice, his paper work on the five guns he kept at his house satisfied the officers and they left, convinced he was on the up and up. One visit was for the original three firearms, and the second visit for the two new purchases. Both times the officers ran all the weapons through their check system.

John wasn't really sure why he was accumulating so many weapons, but he couldn't pass up the deals. He had picked up quite a few items to add to his armory. He considered it good and quit while he was ahead.

There was a lot of unrest in the country, with food availability still marginal and prices high. Another factor for the unrest was the increasing cost of fuel, despite the US holding the Venezuelan oil fields. And inflation was growing faster and faster as money was being printed to cover the costs of cleanup and recovery from the war.

The lack of the illegal, and much of the legal, immigration work force was driving prices up and contributing to the inflation. A few businesses, including the one John worked for, began giving quarterly cost-of-living raises to their employees due to the inflation.

The new Soviet Union was doing no better under the communist rule than they had under capitalist rule. The Soviet Union began dumping gold to buy wheat again, while still increasing its military capability.

The Chinese, having been buying gold for several years for its strategic reserves suddenly quit buying, despite the sudden drop in price. It caught most financial analysts by surprise. John understood how inflation worked, and began turning his slowly depreciating cash holding into gold as soon as the falling price trend became apparent. He knew the downward trend couldn't last long, and it didn't.

In the three weeks of declining prices, John converted seventy-percent of his cash on hand to gold coins, with another ten percent going to silver coins, all through paperless transactions.

When the trend stopped and reversed, it happened overnight, the price going from the previous day's low of $425.00 per ounce, to $1,200.00 an ounce the next morning at the London Price Fixing, after the Asian markets had gone wild after they opened.

PRE-65 SILVER COINS

A week later and the US Congress had passed legislation to restrict the ownership of gold and silver, and recalled almost all bullion forms of both, including bullion coins, at a set price of $300.00 per ounce gold, and $3.00 per ounce silver. The first five ounces of gold, and the first one-hundred ounces of silver, per person, was exempted.

The free market price of gold jumped to $2,275.00 per ounce. The price of platinum and palladium skyrocketed as they were not controlled. Sales records of precious metals retailers were seized across the nation to track down the hundreds of thousands of ounces now in private hands in the United States. Large rewards were offered to those that would turn in those that had undocumented metals.

Only those that had bought the precious metals privately, or through dealers that kept no records, were able to hang on to anything but a token amount. As he had done with firearms, John had a small amount of gold and silver with a paper trail. Ten ounces of gold, and two-hundred-fifty ounces of silver. He turned in his required five ounces of gold and one-hundred-fifty ounces of silver and collected the nominal payment from the government early in the process.

Shortly thereafter a hoarding law was passed. No person or family could have on hand more than a thirteen-month supply of food. Anyone caught with more would have all but a three-month's subsistence supply confiscated for redistribution by the government. That included home preserved food. 'Meat on the hoof' was exempt.

Purchase records of LTS food retailers and buying clubs were used to target 'survivalists'. As with precious metals, large rewards were offered to those that would turn in anyone that they thought had more than 'their fair share' of food.

Though always careful, John became even more low profile than he had been in the past. He made sure his working pantry held under a six-month supply of a combination of LTS and grocery store foods. Some of the LTS food he purchased was on the record, but it was a small enough amount that the rotational use would explain it away.

He was glad he'd been careful. His name did come up in the record search and he was visited by the 'food cops' as they were known. There was some doubt about his use of the food over the period of time he had purchased it, but the several open and partially used cans in his pantry convinced them that he was just a lazy spendthrift and preferred the freeze-dried and dehydrated foods as they were easy to prepare, and cheaper in bulk. After all, he did live in a very cold basement, didn't he?

The draconian gun laws had been for the safety of the children. The precious metals recall was to finance the reconstruction of the country after the war and for the damage the global warming generated storms was causing. The hoarding laws were to ensure everyone got their fair share of the slowly diminishing food supply caused by global warming. Citing the need for stability during trying times, the President, with the backing of two-thirds of Congress, postponed Federal Elections for the duration of the crisis.

Slowly more restrictions on travel were enacted, 'because of the shortages of fuel'. Travel documents were required for any trip more than a hundred miles from one's registered home. The implanted ID chip became mandatory. A Federal monitoring force was set up to enforce the new laws.

When the President announced that the internet would soon be censored by the Federal Government, again to protect the children, the American people were on the verge of revolt.

Too many had been looking internally for month after month as liberties were taken away. Only some, those like John, had been keeping their eyes on the world situation, primarily by shortwave broadcasts, as the news organizations had almost stopped any coverage outside the United States.

All the old problems around the world were still there and beginning to heat up again, one after the other. Most of the world powers began to think of the US as a second-rate power. Many of them seemed to decide to take advantage of that at the same time. But all still feared the ferocity that could suddenly emerge when the nation was threatened.

The Chinese and the USSR had been on again off again 'friends'. They were on again, and both wanted to rise once again to their former glory days. On July Fourth, with two hurricanes bearing down on the Southeast coasts of America, and deadly storms dropping tornados all over Tornado Alley, China and the USSR launched a nuclear missile attack on the United States.

Unfortunately for both countries, several high-ranking members of the US military had planned a coup for the Fourth of July. It will never be known if the President would have commanded the nuclear forces available to her to counter launch. Those in the coup did not hesitate. Orders went out to launch a retaliatory strike.

It wasn't a couple of nukes here, a couple there. Every nation on earth that had a grudge with another attacked them. Those with nuclear weapons used them without mercy. It was worldwide nuclear war.

CHAPTER FOUR

John counted himself lucky. Being in a city that could be a target was an iffy proposition. If caught outside during a nuclear attack, and Tulsa became a target, there was little hope of survival, which was the case when the war broke out.

Not much for crowds, John, as usual, spent the Fourth at home. He was watching a movie when the sound of the Oregon Scientific alert radio sounded off, startling him. He got up from the La-Z-Boy and almost committed a serious error of judgment. John headed for the outside door to take a look around.

But the alert suddenly cut off and the TV and lights all went out at once. "EMP!" John muttered and changed his direction. That might be the only thing happening, but he wasn't going outside now to find out. There wasn't much to do except wait and see. Sitting back down, John wondered what was happening.

He got a glimmering when his RadDetect PRD 1250 key fob radiation alarm sounded for two or three seconds, and then fell silent. A few moments later the basement shook heavily, with a rumbling sound, and small cracks appeared in the walls and ceiling. John's hands gripped the armrests of the La-Z-Boy as he rode out the shake. The shaking stopped, but a few moments later John heard the blast valves on the air intakes and exhausts slam closed.

There was no doubt about it now in John's mind. At least two nukes had gone off. Probably one at high altitude and one in or near Tulsa. That probably meant a lot more were going off, but John could only be sure of the two.

He got up and put batteries in the CD V-717 remote reading survey meter, the CD V-715 direct reading survey meter, and the AMP-200 high range remote reading survey meter. Turning both on, he checked first the CD V-717. Nothing. He didn't bother checking the rest of the shelter with the CD V-715. If there was no outside radiation, there wouldn't be any inside.

But that sudden chirping of the PRD 1250 was bothering him. After a few minutes of thought he paled and sat down heavily. It could only have been the initial burst of radiation emitted during the detonation of the nuclear device. That meant the warhead had been uncomfortably close.

Only very high radiation levels would penetrate the two levels of concrete, totaling eighteen inches, and five feet of earth that constituted the ceiling of the shelter. That meant he'd taken a fairly heavy dose, though it had lasted only a couple of seconds. Much like an x-ray, but probably of much higher radiation. There was nothing he could do about it. The shielding would have reduced the level to less than one forty-seventh-thousands of the outside value. Only time would tell if he got sick.

John clipped on a CD V-742 dosimeter and sat back down, his mind a blank for a few minutes. It had happened, and he had prepared for it, but would the preps be enough? He already had a dose of radiation.

Twenty-one minutes later the CD V-717 began to show outside radiation. John's place was undoubtedly under the edge of the mushroom cloud. The radiation level continued to climb and went off the scale at 500R. John turned the CD V-717 off and turned on the AMP-200. The radiation continued to climb. Finally, several hours later, the radiation level quit rising. The peak was just over 2,000 R/hr and lasted only a few minutes. The level began to fall, though not as quickly as it had risen.

John used the CD V-715 to check out the entire basement shelter. There were no hot spots. There was nothing else John could do. He went to bed and tried to sleep. It was a fitful sleep and John was up early the following morning. He checked the AMP-200. The radiation was down under 100 R/hr and he turned the AMP-200 off and turned on the CD V-717. The readings matched closely.

John breathed a slight sigh of relieve. The dosimeter read slightly over 1 R. But he still had no clue as to how much initial radiation he'd received. He wrote the dosimeter reading down in a journal sitting on the desk beside the survey meters and then reset the dosimeter to zero. He clipped it back onto his shirt and went about preparing a scant breakfast for himself.

The basement had three above ground entrances. John decided to risk a little more radiation exposure to go to each airlock entry and take a look through the small lead glass port in the outer door.

He couldn't see much, but what he did see was devastation. The quadraplex was gone, except for the core shelters, the materials spread out all over the lot in the direction away from down town. The entrance on that side was blocked, but the other two were clear of debris.

John put on his CBRN safety gear and went out to check on the occupants of the quad units. Though the shelters had withstood the destruction of the rest of the quad, there was no one in any of the four shelters. John assumed they had been out enjoying Independence Day festivities.

John went back into the full protection of the basement shelter proper and started his first full day of isolation.

With the PV panel roof of the quad gone, John had to run one of the twin Isuzu 12.5kw power plants to charge the batteries, fed from a pair of 1,000-gallon underground diesel tanks buried and filled one Saturday during the construction of the basement.

The shelter had a large battery bank in the room next to the gensets. Both rooms were vented to the outside, with the combustion air for the gensets drawn from outside, and the exhaust vented to the outside.

John spent his time sleeping; studying; and scanning the commercial broadcast bands, shortwave, and Amateur Radio bands. He was limited to one long wire antenna that had survived the destruction of the quad. Those antennas he'd set up in the huge attic of the quad were part of the debris.

He ate, but sparingly, less so to conserve food, than to an attempt not to gain weight with the sedentary life in the shelter.

The regular sewer line quit working the third day and John switched to using the chemical toilet. He'd lost city water almost immediately after the attack. One of the things he'd had installed on weekends during the construction of the basement had been a two-thousand-gallon concrete water tank. It was kept filled with city water, and a pump pulled from the tank to provide pressure to the house piping. It had continued to work without problems.

He had two 30-gallon portable waste holding tanks into which he could empty the chemical toilet when needed. The portable tanks would be emptied into pits he could dig once he left the shelter.

The shelter was kept ventilated through an American Safe Rooms ASR-100N-NBC filter system.

Buried the way it was, the basement shelter did not need additional cooling than that provided by the earth itself.

John didn't hear much despite his nearly constant monitoring of the communications gear in the shelter. Finally, two weeks after the attack, he began to hear some Amateur Radio traffic on the HF bands. The radiation outside the shelter had dropped to 2R/hr.

He suited up in the Tyvek coveralls, with a Millennium CBRN (Chemical /Biological /Radiological /Nuclear) respirator, butyl gloves, and rubber boots in order to take a couple of reserve antennas out and install them. He also took a quick look around and decontaminated the areas adjacent to the useable entrances of the basement. He tried the Subaru. It wouldn't start. Sometime during his shelter stay some of the quad residents had come back. He left the dead bodies he found where they lay. He couldn't take the time to bury them.

Immediately he began to hear quite a bit more on the radios. He managed to make contact with Adam at his farm on a prearranged schedule and frequency plan. They too had survived. There had been considerably less radiation at the farm and they had been out decontaminating for four days.

There had been heavy losses of the farms stock, but they had enough left, Adam thought, to continue to breed more.

"Okay, Adam," John said. "I'll get out there as soon as I can. May be a while. The Subaru won't start so I'm going to have to go to alternate transport. That means it will take me a while to clear the higher radiation zone. I want to let the radiation fall considerably more before I set out."

"Understood. Check in every other day. We have several operating vehicles. We could come and get you."

"No need to risk it."

"I think you just want to avoid the farm work," Adam said with a laugh."

"Well…" John replied, laughing a little himself. It was the first laugh in a long time.

They both signed off and John tried a few more frequencies. There were operating Amateurs all over the country. John had large US, and individual continent maps and began marking them with contacts he could identify. Some of those transmitting refused to disclose their whereabouts. John couldn't really blame then. Those that were prepared and had survived would most likely be targets for those that had not prepared, but managed to survive through hook, crook, or extreme good luck.

John suddenly thought about Bobby and how he had fared during and after the war. He put Bobby out of his mind immediately. John had serious doubts that Bobby had survived.

Undoubtedly there were other survivors around Tulsa, but he wasn't hearing anything from them on the radios. He fell back into the routine he'd developed in the first two weeks of the shelter stay. According to the spreadsheet designed by TOM of Frugal's Forums fame to calculate stay time in a shelter post attack, it would be another six months or more before he could be out and about with little additional risk of radiation, as long as he avoided hot spots.

That time frame didn't preclude John from suiting up every few days and doing a little close-in scouting and some cleanup on the lot. He kept the time to a minimum, but was able to recover most of the PV panels that had been the south facing roof covering, and his antennas from the attic. John also found the wireless remote weather instrument cluster and put it back up so he could track the weather.

He used some of his in-shelter time to repair the antennas. They were banged up, but not beyond repair with the equipment and parts he had. John also rigged up a set of simple remote cameras to keep an eye on the area without going out.

John's Quadraplex had been the only competed structure in the walled community, besides the display homes. The display homes had not survived the war, either. He saw no one else on his outings.

As summer progressed, John became concerned about the weather. The old adage about checking out things when the smoke cleared didn't seem to be applicable. The smoke wasn't clearing.

From the reports from Amateurs he was hearing, it wasn't the nuclear war caused nuclear winter, for the huge widespread fires predicted by some scientists didn't occur. The overcasts seemed to be caused by volcanic activity. And unlike nuclear winter, 'volcanic' winter was a proven fact.

There had been much speculation before the war about using nuclear devices to trigger geological events, such as earthquakes and volcanic eruptions. Several nations used geological targeting for some of their weapons, in addition to the military asset, industrial production, population center, and resource targeting.

It hadn't worked as well as some had predicted, but a few of the attempts did, despite those that had predicted that it would be a waste of warheads. At least three of the geological targeting attempts affecting the US worked. Mount Rainier was triggered and erupted violently. It added to the atmospheric pollutants.

The eruption of the Yellowstone Caldera was the one that did the most to ensure a volcanic winter. The Chinese targeted three one megaton warheads on the caldera and it triggered the massive eruption.

The third event was as decimating to the country as the Yellowstone eruption. Either the USSR or China or both targeted the volcano on La Palma Island in the Canary Islands. The devices themselves, or the volcanic eruption that they caused, dislodged half of the island. The resulting gigantic tsunami devastated the East Coasts of the Americas from Newfoundland to the bulge of Brazil. The damage was catastrophic for a mile or two inland, to as much as twenty miles inland, dependent on the local geography.

Eastern Oklahoma received its first snow on September third that fall after the attack. The winter lasted into April of the next year, delaying John's departure of the basement shelter till the spring season was evident. He'd planned to leave in February, but the heavy snows prevented it.

He was able to stay in contact with Adam. The Farm had taken in some refugees that had survived the first weeks post war. It had worked out fairly well. What problem they did have was a band of raiders in the area. At the moment, they were fairly disorganized and ineffective, except for attacks on small places. They had killed at least six people since the war and had attacked several more that had run them off.

John had taken the extra time in the shelter to plan carefully. Adam's farm was thirty miles northwest of Tulsa. Before the war it took John about an hour to get to the farm from the city. He was prepared for a full week of travel when he set out. Before he left he removed everything he'd set up outside the basement and stored it inside. He covered all three entrances with debris.

With the basement shelter secured, John straddled the Montague Paratrooper bicycle. Attached was a cycletote.com trailer to carry his equipment and supplies. He set off for Adam's farm.

LOW PROFILE

Instead of the Savage 99 he'd had for its political correctness before the war, John now had slung over his shoulder an HK-91 he had cached several years previously. A musette bag over his other shoulder carried magazines for the 91.

On his hip in a ballistic nylon flap holster he carried a Para-Ordinance P-14 .45 ACP instead of the Colt 1911A1. On the trailer was a Benelli M-4 tactical shotgun. A nylon bandoleer held fifty rounds of twelve gauge shot shells and buck. John also had a pair of pouches from FMCO holding 12 shells each he could add to his combat harness or vest if he needed to.

John was wearing khaki colored 5.11 shirt and pants, with a Cooper Zero Gravity A2 leather bomber jacket, since it was still quite cool for April. Hatch Operator CQB Tactical gloves were on his hands and Matterhorn SAR 12900 were on his feet, with his head covered with an Akubra Lawson Hat. He wore Bodyglove Z87.1 photo chromic safety sunglasses.

The hat, sunglasses, and gloves were in part used to for protection from increased UV-A and UV-B radiation that resulted from the lessened protection of the ozone layer that had been severely damaged by the nuclear detonations. Even with the attenuation of the nearly constant high clouds and ash content of the upper atmosphere, the UV radiation was much greater than before the war.

John took his time traveling, maintaining constant awareness of his surroundings. He stayed on the main roads, working his way around the thousands of abandoned vehicles he saw. There were signs of methodical scavenging of cargo trucks. Not everyone had stayed in the protection of fallout shelters for as long as John had.

He suspected much of the scavenged goods were wasted by those that had scavenged them while radiation levels were still high. Many of the scavengers undoubted died from lethal doses of radiation they received while out in the open.

John stopped at the occasional house close to the road. There were signs that some people had survived the war, but not the winter. He left the bodies where they were. He didn't have the time or wherewithal to bury everybody he found. He wished he was able to do it, for some of the bodies had obviously been partially consumed by dogs that had survived and no longer had regular food sources. He kept a sharp eye out for feral cats and dogs.

He began to see more current signs of the feral animals, as well as wild animals after he got some distance away from Tulsa. He set up perimeter security each night around his camp using battery powered PIR (passive infrared) sensors set up on metal stakes he carried for that reason.

To keep the batteries charged for the sensors, as well as his battery-operated lights and other electronic devices, John kept a pair of Brunton SolarPort 4.4 with BattJack battery chargers arranged on the top of the gear on the bicycle trailer. It took a bit longer than usual with the slight overcast, but they kept him in recharged batteries.

John checked in every evening with Adam using a Yaesu FT-817ND Amateur radio using a compact Miracle Whip antenna.

He ran into his first survivors on his third day out. He was getting close to the farm, but had at least another day of travel. He came upon the small family group as they were out scavenging in vehicles on the road.

When he saw them, at some distance, he stopped and stood straddling the bike. He raised his hand and waved. All five of them, two adults and three children, disappeared behind vehicles. John heard a shot ring out.

It sounded like a small caliber pistol, but John was too busy getting down behind a vehicle himself to really try to analyze the sound.

"Hey!" he called out. "I'm friendly! Don't shoot!"

"How do we know that?" came the man's voice.

"I guess you don't," John called back. "But I am. If you don't want contact, just let me get by and I won't bother you."

"You got any food to trade, Mister?" came the woman's voice.

"Sylvia," yelled the man, "We'll find some! It's too big a risk!"

"If I have some… I'm not saying I do… What do you have to trade?" John asked.

"Tell us what you have and what you want for the food. We'll tell you if we have it."

"Okay," John replied. "I've got six MRE's left that I'll trade. I'll take a tenth ounce gold coin for them, or a roll of silver dimes."

"We don't have any silver or gold!" the man yelled back.

"Your wedding ring," Sylvia said.

"But…" The man fell silent for a moment. "Okay. I've got a fourteen-carat gold wedding band. I'll give that to you for those MRE's."

John didn't really want the ring. He much preferred coinage, or something with real value. But he got another look at the children. They were all standing up now, looking at him. They all looked thin. So did the woman.

"Yeah. Okay," John replied. "Wait there." John went over to the bike and trailer. He opened one of the two Kifaru EMR packs on the trailer and took out the six MRE's.

He closed the pack back up and set the MRE's on top of the gear in the trailer. With his left side turned toward the man, John eased open the flap on the holster on his right side. He wanted quick access to the .45, just in case.

John got back on the bike and slowly pedaled toward the man. The woman and children started toward the man, as well. "Don't try anything," John warned the man. Keep your hands where I can see them or no food. And if you try something, I'll kill you."

The man was upset with the situation, but was holding himself in check. The handgun was out of sight and the man was holding his hands before him. John stopped the bike beside him. "Have the others take the MRE's and you give me the ring," John said.

The man made a motion to the others and they quickly grabbed the MRE's and stepped back. John held out his left hand for the ring. The man struggled with it for several moments before he could get it loose, and it was with obvious reluctance that he set it in John's open palm.

"You know," John said, "I might have given you some food if you hadn't shot at me."

"Can't take no chances," the man said, his fists clenched. "There're a lot of bad people running around. Kill you for your shirt. I'm going to take care of my family any way I can."

"How'd you survive the war and the winter, anyway?" John asked.

"Stayed in the basement of the house," one of the children said.

Another added, "For a long time."

The third chimed in with, "Until we ran out of food."

"We've been scavenging for food since last fall." The man was explaining now, seemingly embarrassed by having shot at John. "Found a grocery delivery trailer and lived off through most of the winter, but some guys came and took it away from us."

"It was still in the trailer? You didn't take it all home?"

"No," Sylvia said. "We started living in a big abandoned motor home close to it."

Again, the man picked up the tale. "The engine wouldn't start, but the generator does. We've been taking gas from cars to keep it running. The air conditioners had strip heaters in them so we were okay during the winter. But it's getting harder to find food and gas."

"I imagine," John said. "Well, if you decide to drift northwest, I hear there is a farm there that gives food for labor on the farm."

The children were trying to get into the MRE outer packs with little success. "I'll let you at it," John said, putting his foot on the left pedal of the bike. "Oh. And here." He tossed the wedding ring back to the man and pushed off with his right foot to get the bike and trailer going again.

"But..." the man said, his voice trailing away, a confused look on his face. John pedaled away before the man could say or do anything else.

John set up his camp early that evening, since he couldn't make the ranch that evening, and didn't see any point in getting there too early the next morning. When camp was set up, John fired up the Yaesu FT-817ND and checked in with Adam.

"I'll be there mid-morning," John said after keying the mike.

"Okay, John. I want you to keep a sharp eye out. That gang hit another place yesterday. They got run off without getting anything. They may be getting desperate for a score."

"Understood. John out."

After eating supper of one of his six remaining MRE's, he took up the HK-91 and scouted around the area. He found what he was looking for and went back into the camp as darkness fell After changing out of the Matterhorn boots for a pair of Cabela's X-tra heavy duty moccasins, John took his sleeping bag out of the tent and headed for the spot he'd found away from camp.

According to the trend he'd plotted using the information from his Brunton ADC-Pro weather instrument; it would be another very cool night. But his Slumberjack Quallofill sleep system was up to keeping him plenty warm during the night without benefit of the tent.

After slipping out of the moccasins, John crawled into the sleeping bag, the HK beside the bag, and the P-14 at hand near the head of the bag. It was just a precaution, but John didn't like to take unnecessary risks. If someone came up on the camp, they would trigger the perimeter alarm. With John outside the perimeter of the camp, he would have a better chance of defending himself if they were hostile, which was likely.

MRE MEALS

John finally fell asleep, waking twice in the night to zip up the sleeping bag slightly more each time. He lay there silently when he woke the next morning, listening. Nothing was out of the ordinary and John went about his normal morning routine.

The bike and trailer packed up and ready, John began pedaling his way toward the ranch, keeping an extra sharp eye out for the gang Adam had warned him about.

It was just before 10:00 AM, according to his Orvis Automatic Field Watch, when John came around one gentle curve in the road and saw a sharp turn ahead. Just around a bend like that would be an excellent place for an ambush, and John knew it. He took the bike and trailer off the road and threw a camouflage tarp over it. With the HK-91 loaded with a one-hundred round Beta C-Mag dual drum magazine, John began the slow task of quietly working his way through the scant woods bordering the road.

He was glad he took his time and kept quiet, stopping after every few feet of advance to scan the area with his Steiner Commander V binoculars. He located five men on his side of the road, all under cover. John couldn't be sure, but he suspected there were at least one or two men on the other side of the road, probably right across the man furthest from John's direction of travel, in a classic L ambush.

John went past the ambush, looking for the ambusher's transportation. He finally spotted it. Like his bike and trailer, the ambushers' old Ford Bronco, and an even older Chevy Blazer. He thought about disabling them, but that would leave the ambushers stuck in the area he needed to pass through. Better to run them off and deal with them later, when he was with a group. He went back through the woods and found a good sniping spot.

For a moment, John wished for the Surefire suppressor he had for the HK-91, but it was cached at the farm. He thought a moment about trying to contact the ambushers first, in case they were not the bandits. But the description of the vehicles that Adam had given him matched the vehicles he'd found.

Finally, no other choice he could think of offhand, John sighed carefully on his first target, the man closest to the point of entry of the ambush. It was a forty-yard shot. A careful squeeze of the trigger of the HK-91 and the man laid dead, a .308 bullet in the back of his head.

Quickly John sighted the next man. Another round at sixty yards and two men were dead. John got up and began stalking the others. There were yells and calls, but none of the men left in the ambush broke cover. It took John only a couple of minutes to get in position to fire again.

It was a longer shot, over a hundred yards, but John again aimed at the man's head, just as he had the other two. The shot was off slightly, but it was still a killing shot, taking the man just behind the eyes. He'd aimed at the ear.

Now, with three shots fired, the remaining ambushers had at least an inkling where John was and began to direct what had been random fire toward his position. John stayed long enough to get off a hasty shot at the fourth ambusher, just visible lying behind a small tree close to the road.

This was a much longer shot and John aimed for center of mass. He fired and scooted before he could assess whether or not he had hit the man. Assuming he lived, he could check later.

With heavy fire coming at his last position, John quickly moved to where the second ambusher lay dead. It was the best cover around and John began to fire rapidly at muzzle flashes. Of course, he was trying to make killing shots, but the main goal was to get the men to abandon the ambush and leave.

With a hundred rounds in the magazine John could lay down continuous withering fire. It took only another two minutes of firing and the ambushers broke cover and began to run toward their vehicles.

John kept firing and downed two more men before the rest disappeared. He got up and cautiously ran down the edge of the forest until he could see five more men getting into the Bronco and Blazer. Both vehicles took off in the opposite direction as John stood and continued to fire slowly.

The Blazer swerved sharply once and slowed down, but then quickly picked up speed again and straightened its course.

John turned back and checked the two men that he'd shot while they were running. One was dead, sporting two widely spaced wounds in his back. One was low and to the right. It was the other round, high on the back, which had gone through his heart and killed him.

The other man was whimpering, trying to crawl away. A quick glance and John saw that his pelvis had been shattered by a series of three .308 rounds just below the man's belt line. John stepped up and drew the P-14. One round to the back of the head and the man was out of his misery. John holstered the P-14 and lifted the HK-91 again.

Being considerably more cautious, John approached the tree where the fourth ambusher had been. There was a blood trail deeper into the woods, and no sign of the man's weapon. Very carefully John tracked the man. He finally caught sight of him, ten yards ahead, limping along, using his rifle as a cane. John sighted and downed the man with a shot to the back of his head.

After confirming the man was dead, which was obvious up close, John went back and checked on the first two men he'd shot. He was sure of his shots, but didn't want to take any chances. Both were quite dead.

Struggling not to be sick at the carnage he'd created, John stripped the bodies of everything useful, and their ID's. Even months after the war, and people were still carrying wallets with licenses and insurance information.

The bike trailer was piled high when John had loaded it with the men's belongings and tied them down. He didn't waste much time getting to the turnoff to Adam's farm. The ambush had been only three miles from the road.

Adam seemed to be waiting for him. "We thought we heard shots earlier. Really faint," he said as John pedaled up to the gate at the entrance to the farm.

"Yeah," John said, pointing with his thumb over his shoulders. "Failed ambush. I got about half of them before the rest ran off."

Adam looked incredulous as he looked over the gear lashed on top of John's set of Kifaru packs. "You ran into an ambush and fought your way out of it? By yourself."

John's grin was feral. "Nope. I suspected an ambush and sniped them from behind. The first two didn't even know what hit them." His grin faded. "At least five more got away. There were at least ten people in the ambush."

"Geez, John! Why didn't you hide out and call for some help?"

Adam saw the surprised look come over John's face. "Adam… I… I just didn't think of it."

"Well, come on up to the house and we'll get you settled in."

Adam walked along side as John pushed the bike up the short road from the gate to the farm proper.

"How are things going?" John asked. "I know you couldn't go into great detail on the radio."

"All things considered, pretty good," Adam replied. "We were in much better shape than the others around here. We were able to pick up quite a bit of stock from some of the other farms that had animals that survived the fallout. The people couldn't really take care of them, so they traded them to us for a share of the food when the animals are processed.

"Several of the people are helping on the farm for food and other considerations. Small amounts of fuel and such. June and her parents are in big demand. They are pretty much the local medical system. Those that can, pay, but quite a bit of the medical work is done gratis.

"You said you've taken in some new people?" John asked, wondering if he would be sleeping his tent, rather than the extra bedroom.

"Yeah. Several. We had to make some new arrangements for live-ins."

"I have my tent," John replied.

Adam laughed. "You don't have to use your tent, Dude." His laughter faded. "It's not much, I know, but we got you a Scamp sixteen-footer. Found a whole double-decker truck load of them. I know they're built to order, so we assumed they were being drop shipped or something when the war started. We don't have the power capacity to run AC to them, but each one has a battery and a solar trickle charger. And they all have water and sewer. These on this end of the line are still empty."

Adam was taking John along the rough road in front of a line of the Scamp trailers. There were nine of them. One fifth-wheel style, three thirteen foot models, and five sixteen footers. Adam was stopping at the third from the end of the line, which was a sixteen-foot Scamp.

"Anyone in the end one?" John asked.

Adam grinned again. "Should have known. Yeah, it's empty. Still keeping your back to the wall."

"You could put it that way," John replied. They walked on down to the last Scamp in the line and stopped.

"We put up another pole barn and made individual storage rooms so everyone could have more space. We moved your preps in. You can stash what you don't need right now."

John nodded. "Okay. Good. Uh…" John had been reluctant to ask this question. "The rental units? How did they fare?"

"Nothing to worry about," Adam said, slapping John on the back. "Everything is ship shape. The manger is a good one. He stuck it out until we could get someone there to lend a hand. Luckily, there haven't been any attempts to break in. A couple of people came and got stuff, but it was their stuff. I don't plan on opening any of the other occupied units for at least another year. Just isn't right. They put their goods in storage in good faith, and I plan to honor that, even though they aren't paying right now."

"You're an honest man, Adam. Always have been. Show me the storage rooms?"

"Sure. The barn is behind the hay shed." The two discussed a few operational aspects of the farm as they walked. "The biodiesel operation is going great. Thanks to you we have the raw materials to make thousands of gallons of the stuff, as long as the oil crops do well. The same with the still. The methane we make from the animal waste provides enough heat to run the still and the biodiesel process."

John nodded. "All your equipment come through okay?"

"We had to replace some electronics in some of the newer stuff, but we either had the parts, or were able to scrounge them. Macon Archelletta's equipment was all in his equipment shed. It's all metal. The EMP didn't affect anything in it. Did a little negotiation with him and got the use of the equipment we need but don't have, to provide him with fuel. And some hands to help. He lost both his regular hands and his boy got a pretty good dose of radiation and isn't going to be much help."

"Speaking of help, I ran into a family on the way in. I told them, not specifically, about a farm this away that might take on laborers for food."

"That's okay. If they find us, we'll have a place for them. We need good family people."

John shot a quick glance at Adam, but Adam continued without noticing. "But having some unattached residents has been a good thing, too. Usually willing to risk a bit more than the family men. And women, when it comes down to that. We had a couple women on their own come into the fold. They are carrying their weight and more. Gotta give them that."

"How many people is the farm supporting now?" John asked as they went into the barn containing the storage rooms.

Adam took a minute to add things up in his head. "Twenty-seven, I think. Be twenty-eight with you. We're supplying the area with meat, vegetables, and a small amount of fruit. We could take on another half dozen workers, with up to ten dependents.

That would let us increase the amount available for the rest of the community, as a matter of fact. We'd be maxed out at forty-four. Anything over that and we wouldn't have as much for the rest of the community.

"Of course, we would need some additional housing to get to the forty-four mark. Water and sewer aren't a problem. Be nice to get electrical power to everyone, but I don't know how we can do that.

"We aren't the only operating farm, but we are the biggest and best organized. Ted Johnson has a going spread, and Macon. Ted has his own biodiesel plant and is good on fuel. Macon just isn't one to take on live-on-site workers. That's why we're supplying a couple for him. Ted took in a couple of families, so he has enough help for his farm at the moment.

"They'd both like to find some greenhouses they could move to their farms. They're a bit jealous of my operation here. The greenhouses really pulled us through the winter."

"I bet," John replied.

Adam had stopped in front of one door in a line of several inside the pole barn. "This one is yours," he told John. Adam unlocked and opened the door into a twelve by twenty-four room. He handed the key to John. "We wired everything we've built since the war, for when power comes back, or we can make our own. But right now you'll have to make do."

LOW PROFILE

"Good planning," John said, pushing the bike and trailer inside the room. He leaned the bike on the stand. Not much light was coming in the open door, even with the large main doors of the barn open. "We'll work on that electrification problem. The house and main barn systems running okay?"

"Yeah. We have power for both of them, between the PV panels and the 12.5kw genset, but that's all we can do."

"In time. In time," John said, un-strapping and picking up one of the Kifaru EMR packs and a leather laptop computer case. He shouldered them and headed back to the Scamp trailer he'd be using.

"Okay, John," Adam said at the outer doors of the barn. "I have to get to work. Get settled and come on over to the house for supper."

"Will do, Adam. And thanks for having this place."

"It's part yours, you know, for having helped out so much. We'd never had made it without your input and monetary help."

John just waved a hand and continued on his way to the Scamp. After he'd put away a few things in the trailer, John went on a self-guided tour of the farm, taking note of the changes and additions. He met and spoke to most of the people working on the farm.

Suddenly the events of the morning caught up with him and he hurried back to the Scamp to lie down for a while, while trying not to lose what was left of his breakfast. It wasn't just the events of the morning, but the total package of stress he had been under during the trip. Constantly on alert for trouble like that he'd run into. Though less than when he was traveling, he'd been under similar stress, being on his own, since the war.

He set his windup travel alarm and lay down on the bunk in the trailer. John thought he would toss and turn for some time, but he fell asleep almost immediately.

John was a bit groggy when the alarm woke him up, but he shook it off quickly as he made his way up to the main farm house. June greeted him enthusiastically, adding her thanks to Adam's for John's foresight to prepare and help them prepare.

He was introduced to Arthur and Hillary Buchanan, June's parents. There were several more people around the large dining table he was also introduced to, but couldn't sort all the names to faces that quickly.

Except for one. Belinda Carlile. She wasn't at the table, but was one of three women helping in the kitchen. John noticed she was favoring her left arm. It seemed to have somewhat limited mobility.

CHAPTER FIVE

Though John was anxious to get to the storage units a few miles away in Hominy, he took another day to rest up from the trip. He kept his eyes out for Belinda, but didn't see her as Adam took him around the whole of the farm to show him what had been done since the war.

"You said the fuel situation is all right. What about transport?" John asked.

"Not bad. Besides the farm equipment and trucks, most of which came through the EMP okay, we have one car and three pickups running on biodiesel, and two cars and a pickup truck running on E85 owned by late comers. They've all agreed to the community use of the vehicles when required. They can buy fuel for personal use for a silver dime per gallon for diesel, and a quarter per gallon E85, since we do have a finite amount of it. Or, they can trade equivalent value of goods or labor over the basic required for subsistence."

"That working okay? Everyone I see seems to be happy. Or as happy as one can be under the circumstances."

"Yeah. For the most part. We have a couple that are always grousing about this, that, or the other, but everyone else keeps it from getting out of hand. Now the outside... That's a different story, as you well know. We've got that one gang really tearing up jack. Though it shouldn't be as bad now that you've whittled down their numbers some."

"Do you think that was all of them, or just part of the gang?"

"From what we've been able to piece out, it was probably only a group. Big part of the gang, but definitely not all of them."

"Been any attempts to root them out? Any idea where they're holed up?"

"No and yes. No to an attempt to root them out, and yes, we have a pretty good idea of where they are right now. That could change now, with your attack."

Adam's eyes had dropped when he'd answered John's question. "We just... We're mostly family men, and well... Just couldn't seem to get a group together large enough to go after them."

John didn't press the point. "Any place they are likely to hit that they haven't yet?"

"Us, for sure. I think it is only a matter of time. But I don't think they are ready to take us on yet, especially after your actions. I'm sure you noted that almost everyone is packing something on their hip. Anyone going very far afield takes a long arm, too, along with a FRS radio. If we need to leave on farm business, a group goes, heavily armed."

Adam shook his head then. "We've had a few make arrangements to use the personal vehicles for trips that went out alone, but they've all been lucky nothing happened."

"What about other farms and small places at risk?" John asked.

"I figure they'll hit the Jones' pig farm eventually. And the MacNameras'. There are a few more people out there that we know about through hearsay, but aren't in direct contact with. I've told Claude Jones and Albert MacNamera we'd sent someone to help if they were attacked and could radio us."

"I take it is reciprocal?"

"Well… sort of. They would try, but each one of them only has three or four people in the family and would be risking everything if they sent help to us. More than one person, anyway, and you know how dangerous traveling alone is."

"Yeah. Guess I can't blame them," John replied, looking thoughtful.

"We think they are holing up between Skiatook Lake and Birch Lake, mostly working the towns on Highway 11, but coming this direction when things get too hot for them there. I'm afraid they probably heard our conversations about you coming to the farm. That's why they were waiting for you."

"I figured they might be monitoring our radio frequencies. That's why I was so careful about things coming here." He looked over at Adam again. "What about law enforcement? You haven't mentioned any at all."

"I know for sure the Sheriff and two deputies are dead. The other deputy is at one of the other farms, still trying to recover from radiation poisoning. He got a really big dose trying to help people. Don't know about State. Haven't seen any troopers. We heard some radio traffic on the scanner a couple of months after the war, but nothing since then. Ditto county radio traffic. Just a little after the war. Nothing now."

"Means we have to handle things ourselves," John mused. "And handle it without risking too many people."

"We do have people that want to help," Adam quickly said. "But they just don't quite know how to go about it. We can't afford to have very many people away from the Farm for very long."

"We'll figure something out," John said. Then, changing the subject, John asked, "Adam, can someone take me into Hominy to get the truck?"

"Sure. Belinda wants to go in and see if she can recover some of her possessions. She got here with the clothes on her back. You should get her to tell you her story. It's amazing."

As they turned toward the house again, Adam added, "I'll send Joe and Dale in with you. Take the diesel Mercedes."

It took almost an hour to round everyone up and get them ready, much to John's dismay. Not because it delayed him, per se, but because it indicated a lack of preparedness to react quickly when something came up.

Belinda was the first one ready, very shortly after Adam talked to her in the kitchen of the house. Adam sent her to look for Joe, and he went after Dale. They had to fuel up the Mercedes as it was showing just above empty. Whoever had used it last had not bothered to fill it when they were finished with it.

John had noticed Belinda had come out of the house wearing a pistol belt with what appeared to be a cut down side-by-side shotgun in a holster on her right thigh. There were two spare ammunition pouches on the belt.

She also wore, John saw, a shoulder holster with some type of semi-auto handgun, with two spare magazines carried under the opposite shoulder.

Joe and Dale too, when they came up, each had a side arm, but there were no signs of spare ammunition.

"Guys," John said, "We're going to Hominy. Don't know what we may run into. I think a little more armament is called for." Both men looked a little sheepish and hurried off to get additional weapons.

"A sawed off, huh?" John asked Belinda while they were waiting for Joe and Dale.

"Yes," she replied. "I can't handle a long arm." She said it matter-of-factly, making a motion with her left arm.

"I noticed that," John replied. "What happened?"

"I don't really like to talk about it," she replied, glancing at John's face for a moment, and then away.

"I understand. No problem."

They stood quietly, waiting for the other two to return. They did so, in short order, each carrying a rifle. Joe had a Bushmaster clone of an AR-15, and Dale sported a Winchester Model 70 in .243 Remington.

John would have preferred a bit more firepower, but said nothing as they climbed into the Mercedes. Joe only had one three magazine pouch of extra magazines, and it looked like Dale had a handful of shells for the Winchester in a shirt pocket.

Dale drove, for John wanted to be loose to return fire if they ran into any trouble, despite Joe's assurance that they had been to Hominy before, without any problems.

John noticed Joe sitting in the back seat beside Belinda. He seemed to be nodding off. Belinda on the other hand, sitting behind Dale, was scanning the terrain on her side of the car alertly.

"We'll pick up my truck first," John said as they neared the town. "Then you and I can go get your stuff, Belinda."

"Okay," was all she replied.

They made it to the mini-warehouse Adam's family owned without incident. Much to John's surprise, after he, Belinda, and Joe got out of the car, Joe climbed into the front passenger seat and Dale said through the open window. "We'll see you back at the farm." And they were gone.

John frowned. He had intended for the two to act as security while he got the truck ready, and while Belinda and he were recovering her possessions.

His attention was diverted when a voice came out of the intercom box at the gate to the walled facility called out, "Advance and be recognized!" and then a laugh.

Not one to take unnecessary chances, despite the man's laugh, John replied, "John Havingsworth and Belinda Carlile. We're from Adam Markum's farm."

"Sure. I knew that. I just always wanted to say that, like them army guys do." He laughed again. "Adam radioed that you would be coming in."

John smiled back as an older man stepped out of one of the smaller storage rooms with a regular door for an entrance. It was the one nearest the gates. John could have kicked himself for not noticing the camera earlier that was mounted under the eave of the building.

He did immediately notice the MP-5SD3 and the shoulder pouch containing six spare 30-round magazines the man carried. The MP-5SD3 went from the man's right hand to his left, as he unlocked the gate. He held out the right for a handshake. "Charlie Smithers."

"Mister Smithers," John replied, shaking his hand.

"Just Charlie," Charlie said, with another laugh. "Unit 93, right?"

John nodded.

"Got your key?"

Again, John nodded.

"Well, I'll leave it to you, then." Charlie locked the gate, turned around and went back into the small unit out of which he had come.

"Let's go," John said. Belinda followed along as John led the way to Unit 93. When they were there, John brought out a set of keys and unlocked the lock on the door with one of them. He lifted the door and they stepped inside. There was just room to move around the pickup truck parked inside. The rest of the space in the 12 x 30 room was stacked head high with boxes of several different sizes, and other containers, including plastic buckets.

"Holy cow!" Belinda exclaimed. "Is this all prep stuff?"

John nodded. "Yeah. The truck is mine, and about half of the boxes. The rest is Adam's." Using another of the keys on the key ring, John unlocked the door of the 1993 Chevy three-quarter-ton, four-wheel-drive, extended cab pickup truck. He pulled the hood release and went around in front to finish opening the hood.

Belinda watched as John reached in and turned a switch. John looked up and saw her watching. "Battery disconnect switch. Didn't want the battery to drain."

"Will it start after all this time?"

"Well, it started right up the last time I tried, not too long before the war. The diesel is doped with PRI-D, so the fuel should be good. It's mainly whether or not the battery has enough juice left. They do self-discharge a little all the time, but these are heavy duty batteries and should have enough power left to start the truck."

John went back to the cab and tried the starter. He hit the glow plug switch and let them heat for a few seconds, and then turned the key. The engine grunted and groaned, trying to turn over. John released the key, turned on the glow plugs again, and then tried once more. It groaned again, but then turned over several times on the starter. John was about to release the key when the engine caught and began to run. He released the key and smiled through the windshield at Belinda.

"We'll let it warm up a bit. I want to load a few things, anyway." John selected several boxes from the stacks and started to load them into the pickup bed.

"I'll help," Belinda said.

John started to decline, but changed his mind. She only tried to move the smaller boxes, and did just fine with them. She let John get the heavy and awkward boxes. It took only a few minutes, and John and Belinda climbed into the cab of the truck. John drove it out of the room and stopped. He got out, closed and locked the storage room, and then climbed back into the cab.

"You'll have to give me directions to your place," he told Belinda after Charlie let them out of the compound.

It was across the small town, but didn't take long, even with their cautious travel. John stopped the truck in front of a small house, the front door standing wide open. "It shouldn't take long," Belinda told John as she was opening the door of the truck.

"I'll keep an eye out," John replied, also exiting the Chevy. "Holler if you need help with anything."

"Okay." Belinda hurried to the house. True to her word, she wasn't inside long. She was struggling with a suitcase when she came out.

John hurried over and took it from her. He hoisted it over the tailgate and set it down. Belinda was going back to the house. She took a little more time this time, before exiting with another case. She closed the door behind her and joined John at the back of the truck. She handed him the case and John put it beside the other.

"Sure didn't take you long," John replied. "Why haven't you come in for your stuff earlier?"

"I had the one case packed. I was planning a trip when the war started. As far as coming before, I wasn't in shape to. In addition, Adam really didn't want anyone off the farm, without a group going. For safety. I guess he thinks you can take care of things alone."

"Don't know about that. But he is probably right. I intended for the other two to stay with us for safety."

"Oh. I thought you sent them back."

John shook his head.

Up to this point, other than Charlie, they had seen no one. That changed as John turned onto one of the main streets, on the way out of town. A group of seven men stood at the side of the road. All had rifles slung. One of them had his hand up, indicating for John to stop. John did so, rather quicker than the man wanted. There was still twenty feet between the men and the truck.

John's window was already down and he leaned his head out. "What's up?" he called.

The man with his hand up took a couple of steps toward the truck. John opened the door of the truck and stepped out, bringing the HK-91 to bear on the men. Out of the corner of his eyes John noted that Belinda had also exited the vehicle and had the sawed-off shotgun up, pointed through the open window of the door on her side.

It caught the men flat footed. Though John knew the doors of the truck weren't much concealment, much less cover, the men were right out in the open on the side of the road. All had automatically put their hands up when John pointed the rifle at them. "Hey! We just want to talk, man!"

HECKLER & KOCH HK-91

"Then talk," John said, ready and willing to fire if any of the men made a move to bring a firearm into play. He took a quick second to look over at Belinda. She was looking all around. John caught her eye.

"I don't see anyone else," she said softly. John nodded.

Again, the man that had raised his hand to stop them spoke. "We're just out scouting for what we can find. You know. Scavenging. Like you guys, huh?"

"We're not scavenging. Just picking up what we already owned before the war," John told the men.

"Hey, look! Everyone has been doing it!" The man began to look a bit panicked and the other men began to shuffle uneasily.

Another of the men spoke up. "We're not stealing from people. We only take abandoned stuff. We got families, man! We have to take care of them." His voice trailed away.

John lifted the muzzle of the HK-91. Seeing him do so, Belinda did the same with her shotgun. "Okay. We're just being careful," John said. "We've run into some bandits recently. Can't be too careful."

A different man spoke then, as they all stir rather unhappily. "The gang is back in this area? We thought they were gone."

"They aren't," John said, stepping around the door, slinging the rifle as he did so.

"We'd better get back home," another of the men said. "If those guys show up while we're gone…"

"I'll take you back if you want," John said.

The group conferred quietly among themselves for a few moments and then all turned and started walking toward the pickup.

"If you would, we would sure appreciate it. We've been gone since early morning," said the first man.

"Get in," John said, motioning to the back of the truck.

The men climbed into the bed of the truck and crouched down, holding onto the grating of the floored cab-over pipe rack. The first man gave directions to their compound. It was only about two miles out of town, but on the side opposite Adam's farm.

Fifteen minutes later and the men were clambering down out of the pickup bed at the gate on a dirt road.

"Thanks mister," said one man after the other.

"Look," John said through the open window, "If you have trouble with the gang, call us. We'll try to help." He gave one of the men a frequency to contact the farm. "Same with medical emergencies. We have two doctors. Their rates are reasonable. It's the Markum farm. You can find us over near Skiatook Lake."

"We heard something about that. Is it true you have food to buy or trade?"

John nodded.

"Any beef or pork?" one man asked quickly, and then added, "We've only got rabbit, chicken, and goat."

"Yes. Again, for reasonable trades or gold and silver."

"We'll be calling on the radio," the first man said. "Thanks for the ride."

John waved and turned the truck around. He looked over at Belinda. "Sorry for the delay in getting you back."

"No problem. We need good relations with everyone we can find."

Belinda looked tired, John thought. "You okay?" he asked.

"Tired. This is more than I've done in a long time. And the stress of thinking I might have to shoot someone again."

"Stress is tough," John replied. "Will talking about it help?"

"No."

There was a long silence as John drove, again keeping a close eye out.

"Maybe it would..." Belinda said slowly, her voice trailing away. She closed her eyes, leaning her head back against the bucket seat headrest.

"I was headed for Tulsa to meet my husband and three-year-old. We were going to fly to St. Louis and drive out to Robertsville to see my parents. Tell them about the baby on the way. Stay there during the scare. They have a place much like Adam's."

John glanced over and saw tears slowly falling down Belinda's cheeks. He started to tell her she didn't need to go on, but she was talking again.

"John... My husband's name was... is... was also John. He had Tabitha with him when he went in to take care of a couple of things at his office in Tulsa, before we flew out. She liked to go with him and pretend to be his secretary..."

There was another long pause, but Belinda began speaking again. "I had a few things left to do. I was always bad about being late. Never being ready when John was. So they were in Tulsa long before I hit the road. I was lucky... When the bomb hit Tulsa, I happened to be looking down at the radio and didn't get flash burns.

"But it startled me and I ran off the road. The car wouldn't restart. None of the cars on the road would. There wasn't much traffic, anyway. People began to panic on the road. Most just started running away from Tulsa, toward Hominy.

"I was afraid to try to run. I have a problem carrying to term... I tried to stay calm and began walking back to Hominy, too. For some reason, I took the suitcase and a couple two liter bottles of water we kept in the car.

"I kept thinking about John and Tabitha and crying. I almost sat down on the road side to just let myself die, but then I thought about the baby on the way and kept going.

"I didn't see how I could make it. The house doesn't have a basement and I figured I'd die from radiation poisoning, but I had to keep going, for the baby. I saw the county maintenance storage yard and got an idea when I saw the front end loader they used to load that salt and cinder mix for the roads in icy weather.

"There were a couple of big culverts there too. They were to replace a couple on the road, but hadn't been installed yet. I'd driven tractors on my parents' farm when I was a teenager, so it didn't take long to figure out the loader.

"I used the loader to push the culverts into an ell shape and then used some odds and ends of stuff to make an elbow to connect them. Then I covered them over with the salt and cinders. Completely on one end of the longest culvert and just made a mound around the open end of the shorter culvert, leaving just enough room for me to crawl into it. I'd just parked the loader when two guys came up.

"Both of them had packs on and were carrying guns. And bottles of booze. They were laughing and talking and drinking. When one of them saw me, before I could get out of sight in the culvert, he yelled to the other one and started running. So did I, but they were too fast for me.

"When they caught me, the older ones said, 'Lady, it is just you're unlucky day. We're all gonna die so the rules don't count.' He reached for me and I guess I went crazy. I was desperate to save the baby, so I fought as hard as I could. They were both already drunk. I managed to break away and grabbed the shotgun one of them had dropped.

"I was lifting it up when the one that still had his gun tried to hit me with the butt of the gun, but I dodged and it hit me on upper left arm. The arm went numb and I fell backward as he started to hit me again.

"My finger was on the trigger of the shotgun when I fell and it went off. The shot hit the guy right in the face and he fell on top of me. The other guy screamed something and came at me again. I don't know how I got the shotgun up again, but I did and fired the second barrel. The shot hit the second guy in the stomach.

"I got out from under the man that had fallen on me and grabbed the other gun and backed away. I watched for a while, but the man I'd shot in the stomach passed out in a few minutes and died right after that.

"I didn't know what else to do, so I dragged everything into the culverts, using my right hand and arm. My left just hung uselessly at my side. The pain really started a little while later and I drank the guys' booze to numb the pain. I guess I passed out, because it was dark the next thing I knew."

Belinda quit talking and looked out the passenger window for a long time. John held his tongue. There was more to the story.

Belinda took a deep breath and let it go in a long sigh. "Three days later I lost the baby. A miscarriage. I guess I just laid there for two or three days, not wanting to go on, but thirst got to me and I began drinking some water again.

"I finally went through the guys' packs and found some food and more water. It kept me going. I remember seeing or reading somewhere that after two weeks you'd be safe from fallout. I'd lost track of days, so just came out when I couldn't stand being in the culvert any more.

"I guess the coyotes had got to the bodies. They were a mess. I made myself search them for more shells for the guns. One of the guns was a pump, I think it's called. I couldn't work it and left it in the culvert. But the two guns used the same shells so I took them all.

"I cut up one of the packs to make a sling for the double barrel shotgun, put everything in the other pack. I reloaded the double barrel and slung it over my shoulder and picked up the suitcase and started walking. I still couldn't use my left arm properly. Doctor Buchanan said the buttstroke he called it, had damaged the nerves in the arm. There wasn't anything he could do. Some of the damage would heal, but it would never be the same.

"Anyway, I got back to the house that evening and just collapsed. I guess I slept for two full days. The next thing I know there are people in the house. I just gave up then, thinking I was going to die, after they'd done what they wanted to me.

"But it was a group from the farm. They were scavenging and found me. They took me to the farm and I've been there ever since."

"I'm sorry," John said gently.

"Don't be," Belinda replied softly. "I've come to terms with it."

"I noticed your sawed off. Is that the shotgun the man had?"

Belinda managed a small smile. "What's left of it. A while after I got to the farm, when some of the newcomers were being trained on weapons, I tried to use it, but I just can't support a long gun with my left arm.

"One of the guys, the Farm's armorer, Jeff Stokes, cut it down for me and made me the holster. He called it a 'whippet.' I do okay with it. I have enough function in my left arm to load it."

"I'm impressed. Most people would have given up."

"I did. Twice. But something just kept bringing me back. I guess what's keeping me going now is the wish to get back to my parents' place."

"Have you contacted them on the radio?"

"No, but they're pretty capable people. There is a good chance they survived. The house has a good basement. Always kept a good garden. The barn is new and quite large for a farm that size. There is also a good chance much of the stock survived, too."

They were getting close to the Farm and Belinda fell silent. John called on the radio that they were approaching and the gate was manned when they pulled up to it. The man waved John through, and closed and locked the gate behind them.

"Thank you for taking me in with you," Belinda told John when he pulled up to the Scamp trailer she pointed out. "And I'm sorry if my story upset you."

"No, it didn't. I feel for you, but you seem to be coping. I'm not sure I could in a similar situation."

"A person does what one must," replied Belinda.

"Come on," John said, opening the truck door and stepping out. "I'll help you carry your stuff in."

John handed Belinda the smaller of the two cases out of the back of the truck and took the larger himself. When she went into the trailer, John set the case he was carrying in the doorway. "Here you go."

"Thank you again," Belinda said down to him.

"Any time," John replied, giving her a casual wave as he walked back to the truck. He drove the truck over to the storage barn and added most of the items he'd picked up at the warehouse to the items already in his storage room.

John parked the truck near his Scamp and carried a box up to the main farm house. John took it into the kitchen when he was admitted after knocking. It was getting on toward supper and June and two other women were making preparations.

"Hi," John said, handing the box to one of the women. "Brought the rent."

"John," said June, "You didn't have to do this."

"Sure I did," he replied. "Gotta pay my way, just like everyone else."

"Oh, my!" exclaimed the woman that opened the box. "The children will love this."

"What is it?" June asked.

"Six #10 cans of brownie mix and cookie mix."

"Oh, John! Thank you!" June said, giving him a hug. "We have all the basics, but I never realized how important comfort foods were until we were in this situation. I should have listened more closely when you were advising us."

"You've done okay, I think," John replied. "If I didn't have a sweet tooth myself, I doubt I would have bought the extras." He suddenly looked chagrined and added, "That's not to mean I want some of the brownies and cookies. They're for the children."

"Of course," June said with a laugh. "We weren't thinking that."

"Well... Good. I'll get out of your hair. Might I ask what we're having for supper?"

"Pork roast, corn, mashed potatoes and cornbread."

"I'll bring my appetite when I come back."

"Just go on and let us get back to work," June said with a laugh.

John laughed, too, and went back to his trailer. He plugged the twelve-volt power cord into the power jack in the wall and plugged the other end into the notebook computer. John turned on the computer and pulled up his supply log. He subtracted the items he'd used the last few days, including the case of food he'd given to June.

He took his time and reviewed all the equipment and supplies he had left here, in the rental in Hominy, his basement shelter in Tulsa, and the other various caches he had. He had the option to go pick everything up and bring it to the Farm, but the thought didn't sit well with him. He put the idea on the back burner in his mind, and washed up before going back to the house for supper.

CHAPTER SIX

John fell into the work routine of the farm quickly and did his share and more. But several things were bothering him and he finally called Adam aside to talk to him.

"Adam, I think we should do something about that gang."

"We haven't heard anything about them since you got here. Maybe what you did ran them out of the area."

"I suppose it is possible, but they've fallen off the radar before, haven't they? After they've hit a place and have supplies to keep them going for a while?"

Reluctantly, Adam nodded. "I guess that has been their MO. What do you think we should do? We have enough to provide pretty good security here at the Farm, but if we pull enough to safely go after the gang, we'd be leaving the Farm almost undefended. There'd barely be enough to keep up with the farm chores."

"I know," John replied, looking off in the distance. "But I'd like to catch them in their hideout. Take them all at once. Before they hit another family or farm."

"So would I," Adam said. "But… I don't know, John…"

"We need to find their hideout first. That won't take a large force. You said you think you know the general area. I'll go and check it out alone."

"No! John! There's got to be a better way."

"You said it yourself. We can't afford to send a large force for any length of time. And a scouting mission is better done with just a few men. Or a lone man, traveling very low profile."

"Any moving vehicle draws attention now," Adam protested. "Your truck will be impossible to miss."

"You're right about that. Did your ROKON come through the EMP okay?"

"Of course it did, but…"

"Be ideal for this trip."

Adam pinched the bridge of his nose for a moment, closing his eyes, and then looked at John again. "I guess it would at that. But I'd sure hate to lose it. Or you."

John laughed. "At least you have your priorities straight."

"I didn't mean…"

"I know you didn't, buddy. I was just kidding. How about it? Be okay to use the ROKON for reconnaissance?"

Obviously not entirely comfortable with the idea, Adam said, "Yes. I suppose so. But you're going to have to promise to check in every day so we can track you and come help if there is a problem."

"Agreed."

The two headed for the equipment shed and Adam rolled out the ROKON. It was used often around the Farm, but wasn't really critical for the operation of the Farm.

Always one to be thorough when he could, John took that afternoon and the following day to check and reorganize his gear, and get the ROKON ready for an extended trip. Since the ROKON could carry more than he could pile on it, John packed heavy. He thought about taking the two-wheel trailer Adam had for the ROKON, but decided against it. He would have much more maneuverability with just the bike.

The ROKON was equipped with sealed wheels designed to hold water or fuel. John filled them with fuel. He also filled two ten-liter fuel cans with gasoline. They would ride as panniers. One of John's Kifaru large EMR packs was loaded for the extended trip, and his Kifaru Marauder was loaded with basic equipment.

If he had to ditch the ROKON and EMR, he could take the Marauder and his weapons and be able to make it back to the farm. He would wear the Marauder and the EMR would ride the seat of the ROKON behind him.

After the bike was loaded, John opened up his topo map of the area and studied it for a little while. John decided that if he was leading the gang, he'd want a spot with a sure supply of water. Like Lake Skiatook. He folded the map and put it away.

With nothing keeping him, John left late in the afternoon after he had everything set up to his satisfaction. Of course, he didn't get very far, but that was all right. He stopped and ate fairly early, and then traveled until he found a good camping spot well off the road. John set up the battery operated PIR security sensors around the camp and turned in.

He was up at five and had fixed and eaten a hot breakfast by six. He climbed on the bike, and headed cross-country toward the nearest point of the lake.

He had to circle the Farm to get to the nearest point of the lake, but he had not wanted anyone to know his plan. If everyone thought he was traveling the roads, so much the better.

The bike was quiet, painted in subdued colors. John too, was wearing muted colors, the same as he'd worn on the trip from Tulsa to the Farm. It would take someone with very sharp eyes and a pair of good binoculars to spot him from any distance.

LOW PROFILE

John took his time, stopping often to use the Steiner Commander V binoculars to check all around. He got to the lake that afternoon and turned northward. Again, he stopped and ate early, and then moved on aways to set up camp.

John set up his perimeter security, but he didn't climb into the tent. Instead he walked down to the water and stood there, letting the last of the twilight fade. He continued to stand where he was, letting his eyes adjust to the darkness, listening as the daytime sounds changed to the sounds nature produced at night.

As his eyes adjusted, he began to again make out things in the darkness that had faded from view as darkness had fallen. And then things further and further away. Finally, John raised the binoculars to his eyes and began to study the shoreline to the north as he listened carefully.

For an hour he watched and listened, but neither heard nor saw anything. He was about to turn around and go back to the camp when a sudden flicker of light appeared on the north shore of the lake. Two more appeared moments later. Smiling slightly, John turned around and went back into his small camp. He was in his sleeping bag and asleep a few minutes later.

There was no way of being sure the lights had been the gang's camp, so John maintained his vigilance as he continued northward the next day. He stopped at noon, as the shoreline turned toward the east. John found a good place to stash the ROKON and covered it with a camouflage tarp.

With the Marauder pack on his back, and the HK-91 over his shoulder, John set out on foot. He stayed in the edge of the trees and underbrush, advancing slowly to the east. Several times John heard something that had him easing out of sight in the woods. But each time either nothing appeared, or John spotted an animal moving just as cautiously as he in the woods.

John heard the camp long before he saw anything. The low drone he began to hear John put off to a generator running to provide electricity. Wary of sentries, John began a search pattern well into the woods and back to the tree line, advancing eastward on each pass. His nose picked up the acrid odor of cigarette smoke.

He took his time following the smell. It paid off when he spotted a man sitting on the ground, his back against a tree, without being detected himself. John eased down and kept checking the man for some time. He would glance at the man out of the corners of his eyes, as he didn't want the man to get spooked by a direct look at him.

John waited long enough to be fairly certain the man was on static watch and hadn't just paused to smoke. John eased up and moved away. He paused long enough to mark his map with the location of the sentry. That done, he continued his search. There were three more sentries, each in a static position.

In John's opinion, they were poorly placed, but that would be good when the attack John was planning occurred. He also found the winding dirt track that led to the camp. It was a new trail. Picking a spot between two of the sentries, John made his way closer to the camp. He finally worked his way to the edge of a large clearing.

It was quite a surprise to find an even dozen large RV's and fifth-wheel travel trailers parked randomly in the open area, amidst several vehicles, mostly older pickup trucks and SUV's. He had his StormSaf notepad and Fisher Space pen out, sketching the layout and taking notes. He discovered that only one generator was running, that one the onboard genset in the largest motorhome.

LOW PROFILE

There were several tents, as well. John spotted five fire pits, which accounted for the flickering lights he'd seen the night before. He tried to get a personnel count, but found it difficult with people constantly moving around. There were several women in the camp, moving freely around. John decided they were part of the gang.

There was a group of four men and two women, however, who were kept under guard as they did various camp chores. John slipped back out of sight when the six captives and two guards moved somewhat toward him. But they entered the woods well to his right. He stayed put and kept silent as the group gathered up downed wood and then went back into the camp.

The sentries changed twice while he was observing the camp. Two of the sentries on-duty came in before their relief went out. They seemed to get a mild scolding from one of the men, but shrugged it off. The other on-duty sentries came in to the camp after they were relieved.

John eased back up to his vantage point and continued to watch the camp until the sun got close to the horizon. It was only when he was about to ease his way back that he saw the large jon boat pull up to the shore, using oars, though the boat had an outboard motor attached. Two men got out and two more got in and pushed off.

John felt a chill go down his back. He'd almost missed the water side security. He'd moved just enough on his way away from the camp to be able to see the personnel change at the shore. He must have missed the other exchanges, if there had been any, which was most likely.

Changing positions, John checked the shoreline. Sure enough, there were two more jon boats equipped with both oars and outboards.

He eased on back and headed for the spot where he'd left the ROKON. He approached very carefully, leery of an ambush if someone had found the bike. But as full dark settled in, John moved forward and uncovered the bike. He stopped and contemplated whether or not to camp there or head back to the Farm for a while before setting up camp.

John weighed the risks of night travel versus being discovered. Taking out the night vision goggles from his pack he put them on and started the ROKON. He eased his way southwest, headed for the nearest road shown on the map. He stopped often, for sounds of pursuit, but heard only the normal night sounds.

When he reached the road, he drove along it for a ways and then pulled off into the woods. He hadn't eaten since breakfast and so chewed some jerky while he set up the camp. With the perimeter security set out, he crawled into the tent and then the sleeping bag. It took a while to relax, but he finally did so, several ideas swirling in his mind.

The next morning, after his breakfast, John loaded up and hit the road. Though the ROKON would do about forty miles per hour, John kept his speed down to conserve fuel, and to maintain a security eye out for problems.

Even with the precautions John reached the Farm before evening. He found Adam and filled him in on what he'd found. Adam called for a meeting of heads of households for the following morning to discuss the matter.

John's spirits lifted a little when he saw Belinda. She was helping in the kitchen again. When he smiled at her, she smiled back.

Being on her own, Belinda was one of the heads of households that grouped together in the main house's large living room. Adam explained what John had discovered. John fidgeted uncomfortably when several of the people congratulated and thanked him for his efforts.

"So," Adam said, "What do we do with the information?"

"Maybe give it to FEMA?" asked one of the women. There were several in the group.

"I doubt they'll be able to help us," John said. "What little we've heard about them; they are only around some of the major cities."

"Anyone else?" Adam asked.

Carl Sutter spoke up. "The smart thing would be to go in and take them out. Do we have enough men to do that?"

"I'll go, too," Belinda said calmly. John started to protest, but several of the other men did first.

"Now wait a minute," interjected Helen Allcot. "Not that all could, or would, there are several of us that are both willing and able to go on such a raid. We'd have to fight them if they came here. Better to take the war to them."

"That's what my wife would say," Chester Hamilton replied. "We both won't go, but she's more than willing and able, as Helen said."

The argument went back and forth, but the outcome was plain. Any women that could and wanted to would go on the raid. The fact that there would be a raid seemed to come automatically during the conversation.

"When?" Adam asked, looking at John.

"The sooner the better, in my opinion," John replied. "I have no way of telling when they might go on another raid, or even if there might be some of them out on a raid right now." John looked thoughtful for a moment, and then said, "Though, it might be best if we put a watch on the camp and hit them when a party goes out and they are at their weakest."

"I don't know," Belinda said. "Seems better to get them all together, if we can. Take care of the problem all at once."

"That would be ideal," John replied. "But we don't know if they are all there now or not."

"I can't believe they'd have more than the twenty-five or thirty men you saw," Carl said.

"From the information we have, where the gang attacks failed or left survivors behind, the raiding parties seem to number between ten and fifteen," Adam told the group.

"I think either way is okay. If we miss some, when they lose their base, they might be easier to take." Belinda spoke quietly.

"What about those on the lake?" asked Helen.

"Good point," John said. "Anyone have a working boat on the lake?"

A rather short man in the rear of the group raised his hand. John didn't recognize him. "I have a boat. But it would take a bit to get it going. It's a MacGregor twenty-six-foot motor sailor. When things got bad, I stripped it and filled it with water. It won't sink, so I had to add a bunch of weight to get it almost completely under the water.

ROKON MOTORCYCLE

"It would need to be raised and cleaned up a little. That shouldn't be that hard."

"Would a sailboat be fast enough to catch those jon boats if they run their motors?" someone asked.

The man, Edmund Whithers smiled and said, "It's a motor sailor. I've got a fifty-horse outboard that will push it over twenty miles an hour. It'll tow a skier."

"I would think that would be fast enough, if we catch them by surprise," John said. "We could go in under sail, and then switch on the motor if we needed to do so."

There wasn't an actual vote, but Adam read the group, after everyone had a chance to speak, and said, "Okay. If we're going, let's go as soon as possible. How many are willing to go?"

June was there as recording secretary. She took down the names of those that said they would go, along with the names the heads of households said that had family members of an age that would probably go.

"I'm going, too," Adam said, "But John will be in charge of this." June looked a bit strained, but didn't object.

After the meeting John and Edmund took John's truck to the east side of the lake. John, liking the way Belinda had handled herself on the other trip, asked her to go along as a lookout while he and Edmund were working. That was in addition to a volunteer that John asked for to go with them. "You know them better than I," John told Belinda. "You pick someone to go with us out of the volunteers."

Belinda nodded and immediately told John, "Sam Johnson is kind of young, but he's very stable and quite capable."

"Okay," John said. "You go find him and the two of you get ready. You'll be in one of the other pickups."

It took two days to raise, clean, and equip the MacGregor. John was pleased when they took the boat out onto the lake and put it through its paces not far from the shore. "This will do," John said. They secured the boat and went back to the farm.

John gathered everyone that was going to go in the barn after lunchtime. He had a couple bales of hay set up for a desk, with his map spread out on it. "Now, the sentries may each pick a different spot than the ones I saw, but there will be a sentry at or near each of these spots."

The hardest part of the planning for the mission was finding enough people willing to ambush one of the sentries. None of the volunteers had a problem going in shooting at the camp, but the execution of the sentries bothered most of them.

Finally, Adam and two others, besides John, agreed to take out the sentries. John would help each one of the three to get into position and then they would all fire at a set time. The rest of the ground crew would begin the assault from the edge of the woods surrounding the camp at the sounds of the shots.

John stressed that they had to be careful of the gang's prisoners, and reminded them that there were some female gang members. That didn't set well with most of the men, but the women seemed to take the idea of killing another woman in stride.

Edmund would have two men with him to engage the sentry out on the lake, and provide some covering fire into the camp from offshore. John went over the plan again and again until everyone could explain their part of the action without a problem.

They left before dawn the next morning, going directly to the track that led from the dirt road in to the camp. Everyone disembarked the vehicles. Sam was to stay out of sight near the vehicles and radio John if anyone came up from either direction. The rest of the team set off toward the camp, following the track at first. Then John led them through the woods, carefully placing each sniper into position, and the rest in good positions around the camp.

John took up his own position to take out the sentry in the most protected position and began a countdown to 1:00 PM. Precisely at 1:00 he fired and his target slumped over with 147 grains of copper and lead in his brain.

John heard the other shots by the snipers. They had not been able to synchronize watches since only John had a watch with a hack feature. They'd figured the offset for the others, but they were several seconds later. John heard at least five shots from the other three snipers and hoped they'd taken them out. He didn't dwell on it, but ran to join the main assault force around the edge of the woods.

He decided to cover the track in and out of the camp himself, in case there were attempts by members of the gang to get away down the track. Sure enough, he barely made it to the track and was running toward the camp when he saw a gang member. John snapped off a shot that missed, but got stopped and had the HK-91 to his shoulder for the next shot.

The gang member was fumbling with a rifle, but didn't get off a shot before John's next shot took him in the chest. John ran up and snatched the man's rifle and threw it into the forest before he continued on his way to the camp.

A quick glance and John saw at least a dozen people down in the camp, including a couple of the women. Belinda's job had been to try to get the captives to safety. John heard her whippet sound off several times and finally spotted her guiding the crouching captives into the woods.

John saw one of the gang members aiming a rifle toward Belinda from around the edge of one of the motor homes and fired two rounds, catching him in the exposed shoulder with the second shot. The man went down and John put a bullet in his head.

He heard a scream behind him and turned to see Chester go down. Spinning back around, John spotted the man that had shot Chester lining up another shot. Firing three quick rounds, John put the man on the ground.

Like several of the others, John hesitated upon seeing the first gang woman that came into his sights, firing a pistol of some kind. But it was only a momentary hesitation. He fired and she went down with a scream much like Chester's.

The firing went on for what seemed like forever. But finally, one and then another firearm went silent. John had given orders that at the apparent end of the battle, everyone was to take a defensive position and wait until John or Chester gave the all clear.

John entered the camp and began checking each vehicle, RV, and trailer. Twice he had people pop up suddenly. One had a gun and John fired, killing the man with a head shot. The second one had his hands up, but John nearly shot him in surprise.

"Get down on the ground, your arms stretched out above your head." He called back over his shoulder, "If this guy moves, someone shoot him."

John continued to check the camp out. Three of the gang lay dead, half in/half out off one of the boats on shore.

Most of the downed people were dead, but there were a few wounded. John was approaching the largest of the motor homes from the driver's side, when someone broke from the side door and ran toward the lake. He was close to the lake and fast. Several people fired at him, including John, but they all missed. He dove into the water and began to swim away.

After running up to the edge of the water, John fired several more shots, but was sure he had missed each time. He looked out further on the lake and saw Edmund motoring slowly toward the shore. John keyed his radio and said, "There is one swimming out! Try to take him alive."

John turned around and continued his inspection of the camp. He found a woman crouching down in the bathroom of one of the fifth-wheel trailers and took her out to where he'd placed the first man and got her down in the same position.

Finally, sure they had accounted for all the gang at the camp, except the swimmer, John called the others in. Helen was tending to Chester. "How is he?" John asked.

"Hit the bone in his upper right arm. It's very painful. I think he'll be okay if we get him back to the Farm for the doctors to take care of him."

"Anyone else hurt?" John asked, looking around at his group of soldiers.

There were a few scrapes and minor wounds. Chester was the only serious one. Edmund came up then and John asked, "How'd it go out on the lake?"

"I think the sentries were asleep. We sailed right up on them. They never knew what hit them. They're all still in the jon boat. We towed it in. Never did see anyone swimming, though."

"So one got a way," John mused. "That might actually be a plus. Maybe the word will get around that it's not wise to mess around in this area."

It was apparent the attackers had caught the gang totally by surprise. Many of the gang had gone down never having fired a shot. Some of the dead and wounded, and all the uninjured gang members, hadn't even been armed. A few that were armed with automatic weapons ate through their available ammunition in seconds. Some of them died, a couple threw down their weapons and surrendered.

"What are we going to do with the gang members that survived?" Edmund asked.

"Adam will have a say, but I'm inclined to pull a jury together from around the area and have a trial."

"Up to me, I'd just put them down like mad dogs," Edmund replied. He glanced over at the former captives and shook his head. "Betcha they would say the same."

"That just may be what happens to them," John replied. "But for the moment, we keep them alive." Seeing two of the former captives headed toward where four of the Farm personnel were holding the captured gang members, John added, "If we can…" John ran over and barely managed to stop the two men from attacking the captured gang members.

"Hold it! Hold it!" John yelled, getting between the two men and the captives.

"I'm going to kill them!" screamed one of the men.

"Get out of the way!" yelled the other. "They deserve to die!"

"They probably will," John said. "But after a trial."

"Nuts to a trial! They should die right here like the rest!"

It took several more minutes to calm the two men down, but finally they went back to join the other former captives Belinda was tending to.

Adam came up to John. He was ashen faced. "I radioed the Farm. They know everyone is going to be okay."

"You all right?" John asked. "You don't look well."

"I never killed anyone before," Adam replied. "Much less a woman... She was going to shoot one of the guys in the back... I've been out in the woods, throwing up."

"I understand," John said softly. "Come on. We need to finish mopping up. I think you should take charge of the prisoners. There are some really hard feelings. They need as much guarding from some of our people as from keeping them from escaping."

"Sure," Adam replied. Anything was better than thinking about what he'd done.

John sent a couple of people back to the vehicles to shuttle them to the camp. He made sure the wounded were sent to the farm so the doctors could take care of them, including the wounded gang members. Next to go were the former captives of the gang. They needed to be seen by the doctors, too.

Belinda walked over to John as he added the last of the arms they'd found to the back of his truck.

"Quite a collection," she said.

"Yeah. At least they'll be on the good side now." He looked around at the various RV's. "I think we solved some of the housing shortage."

Belinda smiled. "That would be nice."

Over the next several days, everything at the camp was taken to the Farm. Word was sent out to everyone they knew about in the area that there was to be a trial for the captured gang members. The prisoners were under close guard around the clock, held in three of the rooms in the storage barn.

Life went on at the Farm, as they waited for the day of the trial. John was awarded the big motorhome, for his efforts dealing with the gang. Those living in the Scamps drew lots to see who would get the other RV's the gang had. Belinda wound up with one of the large fifth-wheel travel trailers.

It took John two days of hard work to clean up the motorhome. The gang leader had been a slob. But he did find a few things he didn't throw out, or give to the Farm, considering them his since the group at the Farm had given him the motorhome.

All the RV units were set near the Scamps and plumbed for water and sewer. Most of the units had gensets. Only the leader of the gang had run his, in the big motorhome, for lack of fuel. With the biodiesel, they had they could run the generators with diesel engines.

John and Adam interrogated all the gang members in custody. None would say much except blame the leader of the gang for everything. All said it was he that had escaped by swimming away. And that he was the only one left of the gang.

The day finally came for the trial. All nine of the gang members, including three women, sat together. Adam acted as judge. John was the prosecutor. Twelve people at random were chosen to be jurors from the people that showed up to attend the trial.

John had talked to many of those in attendance and had a good idea of what the gang had done. He stated the facts he had for the jury, and called on the people that the gang had held captive for them to give their stories.

All of the gang members were allowed to speak on their behalf. All claimed they had been prisoners themselves and only did what they had to do to survive. All claimed to never have killed anyone and had been firing in the air during the attack so they wouldn't be shot in the back by other gang members.

The jury didn't buy the claims. All were sentenced to death by hanging. The sentence would be carried out as soon as arrangements could be made for a gallows. The intent had been to hang them all at once, but that would have taken too long to build the gallows and used too much of the available building materials. The convicted would each be hanged separately. It took only two days to set poles and build the small drop platform.

John gave up trying to find a hangman and took the job upon himself. As much out of tradition as anything, for almost everyone knew who it was, John wore a ski mask while he was on the gallows.

Fortunately, John checked the rope and trap door himself before the executions. He reworked the knot into a true hangman's knot, and made sure the length was correct. He made a couple of adjustments on the trapdoor release so it would open smoothly with the weight of a person on it.

It went as well as might be expected. A few people watched and applauded as the first man went through the trapdoor, the sound of his neck breaking audible to those closest to the gallows. Some turned away sick, some began to question the need for hanging anyone. The three women were the last to be hanged.

Most of the spectators had left by the time the first woman was led to the gallows crying and begging for mercy. It was only John, Adam, and Dr. Buchanan for the last woman. The two men acting as guards left as soon as they'd walked her up the stairs to the platform.

Dr. Buchanan confirmed the last woman's death and her body was added to the others in the slit trench that would be their home for eternity.

It was somber around the Farm for several days after the hangings. All the visitors that had come in for the trial and hanging were now gone.

Something good had come of the event. Adam was able to make deals with several of the other compounds they weren't familiar with for mutual assistance and trading. Some of the groups were poorly armed. Adam was able to trade off some of the weapons they'd captured from the gang for items of which the Farm was running low. A regular trading route would be set up to make the transfers from one compound to another.

CHAPTER SEVEN

Winter came early, as expected, with some of the ash from the Yellowstone eruption still in the high atmosphere. Adam had planned for it and the fields were ready to absorb the moisture the winter snows would bring. John did his turns in the greenhouses, and caring for the animals that winter, but he had a great deal of idle time.

They were essentially snowed in for all of December and January. People went out on snowshoes to check on things from time to time. A couple of snowmobiles were on the wish list for the scavenging team that would go out the next spring.

John took charge of a greenhouse project. They were going through firewood as if there was an unlimited supply. There wasn't, so John was given a portion of the growing space in one of the green houses to start trees from seed for future planting. They were going to be dependent on wood for heat for a long time to come. Ash tree seed were also high on the list of scavenge materials so they could start a coppicing grove of renewable firewood.

Talk of the scavenging operation became more prevalent as spring rolled around. Winter lasted well into when spring should have arrived and the scavenging trips were put off until the field crops could be planted. Everyone capable helped to prepare the fields and get the seed in the ground.

But the planting was finally done, and firewood collection teams were sent out to begin gathering firewood for the next winter, and plant what seedlings they had. Then the plans for the scavenging were activated. There would be three teams.

One team would drop south and pick up US 412 west of Tulsa to see what they could find. It was a major truck route and had potential. Another team would head for Ponca City and then go east to Bartlesville before turning southwest and back to the Farm.

The third team would work Tulsa. At least the parts of Tulsa that weren't still hot. John would lead the Tulsa team. He had some difficulty finding volunteers for the trip, though there were plenty that wanted to go with the other two teams.

John finally told Belinda she could go as a sentry. She'd been pestering him since the planning stages. He got three men to go with him and Belinda. The three men would be in an International bob truck with stake bed with several drums of fuel. The truck would be used to haul things back to the farm. John and Belinda would be John's pickup. The other groups were set up similarly, though with two transports and two small vehicles each.

All three groups left the same day in mid-March. Besides scavenging useful items, the teams were also tasked with making contact with others and setting up communications with the Farm.

The roads were already beginning to deteriorate due to the bad weather and lack of maintenance. John had been able to make fairly good time on his bicycle on the way to the Farm from Tulsa, but the group had to stop often to clear the road of stalled and wrecked vehicles. John's pickup was well equipped to handle the task. He had hydraulic winches in both the front bumper and the rear bumper, along with a collection of other recovery gear. As often as not, John was able to push the blocking vehicle out of the way with the heavy-duty front bumper.

When they did have to use the winches or other gear, Belinda picked a spot where she could see well and kept watch. John made sure the path would be adequate for a semi to get through it, in case they found a semi-truck that would run.

During the trip in to Tulsa they didn't see anyone. But as they got into the city proper, people began to appear. John had insisted everyone wear a dosimeter to keep track of accumulated dosage of radiation. He had also had a CD V-715 with him to monitor the radiation levels still existing close to the ground zero of the Tulsa device.

If the people they were seeing were staying in the areas where John and the others saw them, they should be all right, radiation wise, for the level was quite low. But if they were venturing into Tulsa deeper, they were putting themselves at great risk. John and his people would be going into some of those same areas, but their level of exposure was quite low to start with.

John had insisted some good will supplies be brought along. Between handing them out in exchange for information, and giving them directions to the Farm so they could trade for food or whatnot, John got quite a bit of useful information.

While the survivors they saw had done quite a bit of scavenging, it had not really been organized, and for the most part they had stayed away from the crater. John had a plan, and it involved getting as close to the crater as the survey meter indicated was safe. The three men and Belinda had all agreed to work in as high as 2R/hr of radiation for a day at a time.

Using a phone book, they picked up at a payphone, John mapped out the path they would take. It would allow them to search the outer reaches of the city and make forays in toward the crater when they were close to a place John wanted to search.

Things went a bit slowly at first, the three men seeming quite reluctant to break into places that were locked up. Part of it was the finding the occasional dead body in protected places where animals couldn't get to them. The probability of running into the dead was one reason John had insisted all the members of the team take and use protective masks and goggles. If anyone didn't have any, it was the first thing they were to look for.

The three men were disappointed they weren't finding much of use or value in the beginning, but their spirits picked up on the first run in toward the crater. They went to a gun store John had noted in the yellow pages. It had been hit by other scavengers. From the look of it, the scavenging had taken place right after or during the war. There were still many firearms left, but they'd obviously been picked over and the choice ones taken.

At least, the choice ones someone not knowledgeable about weapons would want. There were plenty of useable weapons and John and the men loaded them all into the International. What really amazed John was the fact that those that had taken the guns had apparently only taken a few magazines' worth of ammunition.

There were still a good number of magazines suitable for the weapons at the Farm, and several cases of ammunition. The door to the back room of the gun shop wasn't immediately obvious. It was still locked. When John used a sledge hammer from the truck to open it, they found more guns, accessories, and ammunition. All of it, too, went onto the International.

The agreement Adam and John had made with all those going on the scavenging expeditions would each get a portion of the take. Anything they wanted. Even though they had essentially just started, all three of the men with John immediately laid claim to a couple of weapons and ammunition for them.

The next few days netted a little food, quite a bit of liquor, some tools useful for the farm, and something John knew many of the women would appreciate. Bolts of cloth and sewing supplies. John also made notes of the location of things that the Farm could use, but he didn't want to take up space in the International just yet.

They worked for two weeks, camping each night in low radiation locations, until the bed of the International was full to overflowing. John sent the three men back to the Farm with the load. John told Belinda she could go with them, and that he was going to continue scrounging until the pickup was full, or he ran into trouble. Belinda opted to stay with John.

John's agreement with Adam had been different from the others. He got a share of everything that was found by his team, plus could keep anything he found on his own. Once the others were on the way back John turned the truck around and began to back track their route.

"Two reasons," John said when Belinda asked him about it.

"One, someone has been shadowing us and I want to find them before he, she, or they, decide to do something. Plus there are a few places I want to hit on my own." John looked over at Belinda. "We can stop anywhere you want, too, if you want to look through the yellow pages for something of interest. Just as long as we can get it into the truck."

The thought of running into someone antagonistic didn't seem to bother Belinda, John saw, as she looked thoughtful for a minute. "Yeah. There are a few things I'd like to find. I'll look through the yellow pages this evening."

With that settled, Belinda began keeping an especially good lookout. There'd been five sets of eyes before. Now there were only two, and Belinda was sure that if John thought someone was following them, it was true.

John took a fairly direct route to the first spot on his list. He had to move several vehicles using the winches before he could get to where he was going after they left the route they were back tracking.

It was the largest of the coin shops that he did business with acquiring his gold coin and silver coin holdings. John wasn't surprised to see that it had been broken into. He parked the truck and he and Belinda got out.

"I'll check it out while you watch, and then you can come in and get anything you want while I keep an eye out."

"Really? Isn't this looting, not scavenging?" Belinda asked from the perch she'd taken on the top of the overhead rack.

"It is if you think it is. I don't."

"Okay," Belinda said. "I was just asking."

John grinned up at her. "No problem."

He stepped through the broken glass of the front door and entered the shop. John shook his head. He wasn't surprised to see that not only had the display cases been ransacked, they'd also been trashed. Turned over, the glass broken, drawers out. Just about everything but pennies and nickels had been taken from the cases.

John bypassed the showroom area and headed for the back. It too had been ransacked and there were obvious attempts to get into the vault. It was intact. John smiled and went back to the truck.

"My turn now?" Belinda asked. "Though you aren't carrying anything."

LOW PROFILE

"No, actually. I'm just getting started," John said, tilting his head up to see her. "Would you unfasten that bundle of pipes for me?"

Belinda did as requested and handed him two of the tubes when John asked for them. "Thanks." John got a portable gas welding outfit out of one of the tool boxes of the truck and carried it and the tubes into the shop. Belinda went to watching around the area again.

John hooked up the second oxygen line from the tanks to one of the tubes and set it down. He lit the cutting torch with a striker and then held the flame to the open end of the tube, after turning on the oxygen to it.

With the thermal lance burning white hot, John attacked the vault locking mechanism. It didn't take too long. When he had cut completely around it, using up one and a half of the lances, he shut the oxygen off to the lance and let it go dead. He stepped back and shot a hard kick into the locking dial. It fell through the door into the vault.

John had to manipulate the locking handle a bit to get the locking lugs to retract, but he was finally successful and opened the vault door.

"Well, nuts!" he said softly. The owner of the shop, his wife, and two children lay dead on the floor of the vault, beside a pile of supplies and another pile of trash. The smell of the improvised toilet was terrible.

John didn't waste time. The shelves didn't have much on them. Alfred had told John on John's last visit, that he would be closing the shop soon and moving to Houston to open a new shop. He'd been letting his inventory go down for several months. Most of what he had left was on display.

What hadn't been on display were the bullion metals. It wasn't a big part of his business, but there was a small steady market for coins, rounds, and bars of gold, silver, platinum, and palladium. John quickly took the tools back to the truck and loaded them up, telling Belinda, "I won't be much longer."

He took a brown leather teardrop shoulder bag from behind the front seat of the truck and went back into the shop and then the vault. He took it all. There were only a few pieces of platinum and palladium, and John doubted their value in the current situation, but he took them anyway.

Mostly he was interested in the Gold Eagles and Buffalos, and pre-1965 US silver coins, with gold bars, silver rounds and bars secondary. But he took them all.

The shoulder bag though a long way from being full, was heavy. John carried it out to the truck, put it behind the seat, and told Belinda, "Your turn. Afraid I didn't leave much." Then more softly, "Be aware, it isn't pleasant in the vault."

"Is it really worth my while to go in?" Belinda asked.

"Actually, no. I cleaned out everything I think is of value. But you might find something you like, among what's left."

"I'll just take your word for it. I have my own spots I want to hit." Belinda climbed down from the truck rack and got into the passenger side of the pickup while John got in the other side.

"It's getting late. We'd better get back to safer ground and find a place to camp."

"The same place we camped yesterday? It's close."

John shook his head. "Not with just the two of us. There was some security in numbers. With just the two of us we must be more careful. It will be a meal in one place, and a camp in another."

"Oh. Okay. I trust your instincts," Belinda said, watching the terrain on her side of the truck.

They had been setting up tents for their camps, but John found a location he liked with a house on it. It was a lone house, off by itself. The houses around it had all burned during or after the war. John and Belinda carefully checked it out and then set out the perimeter alarm system, with the truck inside the perimeter.

"You pick a room and I'll take one opposite you," John told Belinda as they carried their packs into the house.

"Well, not to be a chauvinist," Belinda said with a grin, "but I'll take the master bedroom."

John laughed. "That's fine. I'll set up in the living room."

Belinda had started down the hallway to the master bedroom, but turned and asked, "This is a security move, isn't it? If whoever is tracking us tries to attack they can't catch both of us off guard."

With a small smile, John said, "Very good, Belinda. That is why we're here, instead of a camp." She nodded and they each went to turn in, weapons always handy.

The next morning it was raining heavily when John woke up and took a walk around the area. He was making breakfast for them when Belinda came into the living room, dressed and ready.

"Raining," she said, taking the cup of coffee John handed her.

"Yeah. From the looks of it, we should be able to make a short run by noon or so. Did you find some place you wanted to check out?"

"Yes. A couple." Belinda got the phone book and showed John an address. "If this isn't in too hot of an area?"

"Big mall, huh. I don't know. We'll just have to check and see." He looked over at Belinda. "I'm willing to push the limits a little, if we need to. If you are."

"It's important to me," Belinda said simply.

"Okay then."

"I may need quite a bit of space for boxes," Belinda said, rather tentatively.

"There is plenty of room left in the truck. And there is some space on the overhead rack. You can use it all."

"Thank you."

John smiled and said, "No problem. I'm going to clean my weapons, if you'll keep an eye out."

Belinda nodded and strapped on her holsters.

As the rain continued, each cleaned their weapons and made minor adjustments to their equipment. After a light lunch of jerky and gorp, they gathered up the perimeter warning devices, stowed them, and then headed for Belinda's mall.

The radiation was significantly higher than the 2R/hr they had planned on exposing themselves to. The radiation level at the mall was still 5R/hr. "We have to limit it to five hours," John said. "I don't want to risk more than that."

"That should be enough."

"You want me to check things out first?" John asked.

Her "No" response didn't surprise John. "I'll be careful."

"Okay, call me if you run into something."

Belinda touched the Motorola FRS radio in the pouch on her belt. "I will, don't worry."

John wondered around the outside of the mall, checking carefully for potential surprises. They had parked in an area of the parking lot with few vehicles, for security. John checked out the vehicles nearest them. All were abandoned.

Belinda came out a few minutes later, pushing a handcart loaded with boxes. John noticed she looked a little green. "Bad?" he asked, suspecting the reason.

"Yeah. It looks like a lot of people were caught here and tried to make it through. Doesn't look like any made it. But there are signs of scavenging. Can't tell if it was the people left here, or scavengers like us that came in later."

"If you want," John said as he loaded the boxes into the truck, "you can tell me what you are picking up and I'll do it for you."

"No," Belinda replied slowly, visibly tempted by the offer. "No. I need to do this myself."

"The offer stands," John replied, "If you change your mind."

"Thanks," Belinda said, heading back to the mall entrance, pulling the handcart behind her.

Belinda made dozens of trips. John could see her tiring. "You sure you don't want me to take a turn or two for you?" John asked when Belinda sat down on the tailgate of the truck to catch her breath.

"No. The five hours are almost up. I'll just make one more trip and we can go. The truck is almost full, anyway. I wanted to hit that big pharmacy today that we passed coming in, too."

"Okay," John replied. "I'll start strapping things down."

Belinda was struggling to keep the huge load balanced on the handcart when she returned. John smiled and ran to help her. "You made quite a haul," John said as he attached the last hook of the spider net cargo webbing to a tie point on the bed rail of the truck.

Tiredly Belinda nodded. "Yeah. I'm beat, but it'll be worth it to get this stuff back to the Farm."

They climbed into the cab of the truck and John headed back the way they had come. He didn't like to back track. It was a risk. But Belinda wanted items from the pharmacy.

The pharmacy was in a much lower radiation area. "Take your time," John said.

Again, Belinda made several trips, this time with a shopping cart. "It's been ransacked," she told John on her first trip. "But I'm finding the things I want."

Belinda stood watch after she'd moved everything she wanted so John could check the place. He headed for the pharmacy proper. Belinda was right. The rest of the store was a jumble, but the pharmacy was really a mess.

John took his time and gathered up every medication left that he thought would have any use to those at the Farm. John was working from memory. The doctors had sent a list and the group had hit pharmacies earlier, gathering everything they could find. But John thought there could never be enough, so he took what he could find. He also cleaned out the first aid supplies, which had been hit, but not too badly. When he was done, there wasn't a square inch of space left in the truck.

"Farm," John said, "Here we come." He and Belinda were back in the truck and John pulled out onto the street. "I know you're tired," John said to Belinda, "But I'd like to go ahead and go all the way back tonight. We've been pushing our luck."

"You think someone is still tracking us?"

"Yes, I do. I've seen movement out of the corner of my eyes twice. It very well could be different individuals, but I don't want to take a chance. I doubt anyone knows what we have, but a loaded truck like this is going to be a tempting target."

Belinda managed a small laugh. "They'd be really disappointed in my stuff."

John looked over questioningly.

"Women's stuff. A lot of us are lacking in some of the niceties. We picked up a lot of necessities for women during the group work, including some of the same things I got, but not everything I know some of the other women would like to have.

"I owe several of the women on the Farm favors for small things they've done for me. I'll give them some of what I picked up. Some of it is for me, so I don't have to use up common stores. The rest I'll use for trading. Things like bras and panties. Some make up. Condoms. Feminine hygiene supplies. Things that aren't critical, but help women feel better about themselves."

"That's good," John said. "Makes me feel bad about my rather mercenary perspective on scavenging. If I'd thought about it, I would have looked for some of the same things, just for trading."

"I don't believe that. You've been helping out more than your share. Adam and June occasionally mention things that you are responsible for the Farm having, either by providing yourself, or making it known that something is important so they could acquire it."

"You have to remember; it was all in my self-interest."

"Okay," Belinda said softly. "Have it your own way. Just don't think you can fool me."

John had no response and they drove along carefully. When it got full dark, John didn't turn on the headlights. He took out the night vision goggles and put them on. Belinda found it eerie to be staring out at the dark while John drove at what seemed a perilous speed.

"Won't they see brake lights?" Belinda asked after John had to brake and maneuver around an obstacle.

John patted the console between the custom bucket seats. "I have cutouts on all the lights inside this panel. The brake lights don't show."

"Oh. Clever."

"Consider me paranoid."

"Just because you're paranoid doesn't mean they aren't out to get you," Belinda said, quoting the old joke.

Both laughed and then fell silent as John concentrated on his driving. John called the Farm on the radio when they got close, to let them know he and Belinda would be there shortly. It was Adam at the gate when they arrived.

"You bring everything in Tulsa that was left?" Adam asked, shining the five-cell Maglite beam over the contents of the truck.

John laughed. "Not hardly. There's plenty left for a few more runs."

"I'll just have to take your word for it. Come on through and I'll lock up behind you."

John stopped the truck in front of Belinda's fifth-wheel trailer and let her out. "See you in the morning. I'll park the truck in the storage barn, just in case it rains here. We can unload after breakfast."

"Okay," Belinda replied. "I'll see you in the morning, not so bright and early."

Again, John laughed. "Good point. I may just sleep in myself."

Belinda didn't object when John began to help move her boxes from the truck to her storage room in the storage barn. "Leave that one out, please," she said when John picked up one of the last of the boxes. "I want to take that one and this one to the trailer," she said, hefting the last box. The two boxes had been the first ones she'd brought out of the mall.

John ran Belinda and her two boxes back to her trailer, and then drove up to the main house. June greeted him at the door. "Welcome back."

"Hi. Got some more medications and first aid supplies for the Docs." June helped John carry the boxes inside. John then asked, "Is Adam around?"

"He's out and about somewhere."

"Just tell him I was asking for him, if you see him before I do."

"Okay. How was the trip?" June asked, halting John's move to leave.

"It went fine," John replied, looking slightly puzzled. "Didn't you see the inventory sheets I sent back with the bob truck?"

"I saw it. What about after bob truck started back?"

"Fine, too. I found a few things I was looking for, and so did Belinda. She'll probably tell you about them." Again, June stopped John from leaving with a question. "I assumed that. What about Belinda? How'd she do?"

"Great. She's a real trooper. Held up her end and then some."

"I see. You like her, I take it."

John finally saw where the discussion was going and actually blushed slightly. "Uh. Yeah. I like her fine. Look, I really do need to go find Adam."

June was grinning at John's back when he went out the door, shaking his head as he went, muttering something June couldn't make out.

John found Adam in the animal barn, checking on some of the livestock. The Farm didn't have a real vet. Adam was the closest thing they had to one. He'd been going to school to get a vet degree when his parents had died in a plane crash and he came home to run the farm.

"What's it look like?" John asked, coming up on Adam just as he slapped a hog on the rump to send her trotting out to join the others in a pasture.

"She's fine. It was her first litter and it was a big one. She struggled some at first, but she's doing fine now."

Adam and John walked out of the barn and stood at the pasture fence to watch the animals.

"Got something for you," John said after a few minutes. He took out a small, red nylon ditty bag and handed it to Adam.

Adam opened it and looked inside. He tried to hand the bag back to John, but John wouldn't take it.

"It's the farm's share of the take."

"John," protested Adam, "what you found after the official Farm scavenging operation is yours. You don't owe the Farm anymore."

"Sure I do. You are providing a safe home base for me."

"And you are doing your share."

"Just consider this part of doing my share. The Farm can't supply everything we all need on its own. We are going to have to barter and buy some things. For those that will take it, gold and silver are the best way to do a transaction. If we do it, maybe a lot more will start."

Adam sighed. "Okay. You win. What is in here?" he asked, opening the bag again.

1 OZ. American Gold Eagle Coin

"Only two each one-ounce, half-ounce, and quarter-ounce gold Eagles. four tenth-ounce, and a dozen one-ounce silver Eagles. And believe me, I kept more than I'm giving you. A lot more."

"I'll certainly add it to the Farm's coffer, if you insist. Thanks. What do you have planned next?"

John looked a little taken aback. "What do you mean?"

"You've always got something brewing in the back of that mind of yours. I was just wondering what might be next on the agenda. No offense, John. Really."

John smiled. "None taken, Adam. You just caught me by surprise, is all. I hadn't really thought that far ahead, except for generalities." John paused, and suddenly grinned. "Okay, I guess I do have some plans.

But none for the near future. I'll just be helping on the farm for a while."

"Okay," Adam said, slapping John on the back before he headed for the equipment barn to see what he could do to help out that day.

After supper that evening at the main house, where Belinda was once again working, John took her aside and asked her to stop at his motorhome when she was finished with the clean up.

When she knocked on the door, John let her in. She immediately saw why he'd asked her in. It wasn't romance. It was weapons related. Laid out on the dinette table was a carbine and its accoutrements. She looked up at his face. John had a serious look on his face.

"I thought you might be able to use this," he said, motioning toward the semi-automatic version of the Steyr AUG. "Being a bull pup, you don't have to support a lot of weight with your left arm. Give it a try."

John picked up the carbine and handed it to Belinda. Her eyes lit up as soon as she had it in her hands. "Oh! Wow! Yes. This is great. How much does it kick?"

"It's .223 so it is going to kick much less than your whippet. I think you'll like it when you shoot it. I thought you could take it with you and familiarize yourself with it tonight, and you could practice with it tomorrow sometime."

"That would be great." Belinda lifted her eyes up to John's. "Thank you."

John smiled back. "Sure thing. No problem." He began to point out the various other items on the table. "There are twenty thirty-round magazines for it. That will let you rotate loaded and unloaded magazines to avoid stressing the springs. A couple of triple magazine pouches, cleaning kit, sling, a dump pouch for empties, a manual for the AUG." John pointed to the floor under the table. "And a thousand rounds of ammunition."

"What do I owe you for all of this?" Belinda asked.

John immediately shook his head. "Nothing. It's for all your help on the scavenging run. Your whippet is great for close in, but I wanted you to have some medium range firepower, just in case."

"Oh. Well, okay, I guess," Belinda replied slowly. "I do prefer to pay my own way."

"I know. And you are. You're willingness and ability to act as sentry is payment enough."

John put everything on the table in a box sitting on the bench seat of the dinette. Belinda slung the AUG over her shoulder and picked up the box while John picked up the crate of ammunition.

"Let's get it over to your trailer so you can check it out."

John was whistling when he walked back to his motorhome.

CHAPTER EIGHT

They made three more scavenging runs to Tulsa during the summer. The last two concentrated on the train yard and harbor. There they found three semi-trucks that would start. It really paid off. They were able to move whole truckloads of products from the site to the Farm. There were far more items there that they had no use for, than items they could use, but John dispatched twenty-three trailer loads of usable items to the Farm.

John kicked himself mentally for not hitting the place sooner. The semis would have made the other scavenging trips much easier and productive. John and Belinda continued to scavenge for themselves. Neither told the other that they were each also filling requests from residents at the Farm for specific items.

It was on the last trip before winter when they ran into trouble. John and Belinda had been keeping a careful watch, leery of being ambushed, but despite the feeling they were being watched from time to time, no one had tried to interfere with their work.

Some of the survivors in and around Tulsa began to make contact with the scavenging team. Many of them were in poor shape. But John authorized some trading, to get them some fresh food, mostly in return for information.

John felt vindicated when information started coming in that there was a bandit operating in the area. No one was certain there weren't more than one, but most of the reports were similar and John believed it to be one, or at most, two people actively preying on others.

Mostly whoever it was struck in the middle of the night, taking primarily food and weapons. But he didn't hesitate to kill if he was resisted. There were reports of a couple of attempted rapes at gunpoint, but in both instances the man ran off before he actually did anything.

John was especially leery when they found a boxcar full of packaged food items. Many of the canned goods were ruined because of the severe winter. The cans had frozen, burst, and then leaked when they thawed out. That ruined some of the paper packaged items, but well over half of the carload was useable.

As soon as they discovered it, John set Belinda up in a secure spot to keep a good eye on their surroundings. They only had one semi to load. The other two were already making runs back to the Farm. The truck was pulling away from the boxcar when John's FRS radio sounded.

"I think we have a visitor. He disappeared on the other side of the string of cars you're working." Belinda's voice was low coming through the radio speaker.

John squatted down and took a quick look under the railroad cars. He didn't see anything, but he trusted Belinda. He moved the HK-91 into a ready position and began to ease beneath the boxcar to get to the other side.

He heard the three loud pops from Belinda's AUG and flattened himself on the ties between the rails under the boxcar. He still hadn't seen anything. But suddenly there was a burst of auto fire from somewhere close to him. John heard Belinda fire three more times, and then heard running feet, moving away from him.

John scrambled from beneath the boxcar, on the far side, and brought the 91 up. But he only caught a glimpse of a body running around the end of another string of cars some distance away. John lowered the rifle and then headed for Belinda's position.

"You okay?" he called up to where she was perched in one of the enclosed traffic control towers that were located at various points in the yard.

Belinda began to climb down the ladder. "Yeah. I'm okay. But he sure scared five years off my life. I thought he had you."

"He wasn't shooting at you?" John asked. He hadn't heard any impacts of bullets close to him when the man had fired.

"No. Fortunately he moved into the opening between two cars after the first burst and was sighting on where you were, I guess. I don't know if I hit him or not, but he took off running."

"Yeah. I caught a glimpse." John looked at Belinda when she was on the ground. "Thanks. He might have got me without your help."

"Like you said. Goes with the territory," Belinda replied with a slight smile. The smile faded and she asked, "What do we do now?"

"Not much to do. It's too dangerous for me to try and track him. I don't want to give up these supplies. We just maintain a watch from a secure position. I'll set up the perimeter alarms. You might as well climb up inside and try to get some rest. We'll be swapping watches all night."

Belinda got their sleeping bags from the truck and made a nest for herself in the boxcar while John set the alarms. After the alarms were set, John opened the door of the boxcar facing the one with the supplies. He climbed inside closed the door down to just a crack from which he could keep an eye on the other boxcar, using the night vision goggles.

It was nearly midnight when Belinda eased out of her comfortable position and left the boxcar. When John saw her, he opened the door of the boxcar he was in. John removed the night vision goggles and gave them to Belinda. When she was in the boxcar, set, John went to the other car and made himself comfortable. He set the alarm on his watch to 4:00 AM and went to sleep.

Nothing had happened by six when John started breakfast for them. He'd taken the last watch at four. He let Belinda sleep until she woke up on her own a little after 6:30. She took the cup of coffee from him when he held it out, and then sat down on the tailgate of the truck to drink it and eat breakfast.

John wandered around the yard after breakfast while Belinda kept watch from the second boxcar. Taking great care, John tried to find the man that had attacked them. He gave up and went to join the others when two of the semis showed up.

The remaining good items in the boxcar fit into the two semis, and John sent them on their way, with a caution to keep a sharp eye out. After the semis left, John and Belinda repacked the pickup and left the train yard. They debated on whether or not to continue scavenging on their own for a little while, or go directly back to the Farm. The final decision was to keep scavenging in a fresh area of the city. They would also try to set up an ambush if seemed that they were being followed again.

"How did the AUG handle?" John suddenly asked Belinda, as he drove toward a huge open air strip mall, this time on the east side of the city. "Great!" Belinda replied enthusiastically. "It's the perfect weapon for me."

John smiled over at her. "But you'll keep your whippet and side arm, too, I take it."

"Yes," she replied, smiling back at him. "The proper tool for each job."

It turned out that the radiation was almost 5R/hr at the mall, so they would have to limit their time there. But since they were only seconds away from the truck, and could keep it in sight through the big front windows each store in the mall boasted, they could each search a store at the same time.

John gave Belinda first choice and she chose another pharmacy. Apparently because of being downwind and receiving heavy fallout, the mall showed little sign of having been scavenged. The stores did show the effects of having a horde of panic buyers inside when the war started, but other than food, water, and booze, most of the stores were still well stocked.

While Belinda gathered the items she wanted, John hit the pharmacy proper. He was able to substantially add to the Farm's supply of medications. Next they hit a large coin shop in the mall. It was one of the stores that had been looted during the initial hours of the attack. But like the other coin shop John had found, the vault was still locked up tight. Fearing a little what he might find, he burned the locking mechanism out with a thermal lance. He sighed in relief. There were no dead bodies.

Belinda had been keeping watch outside since John had needed to concentrate on the thermal lance while he was using it. They both returned to the vault after John had taken the gas welding set back to the truck and secured it. It took only a few minutes to gather up everything of value in the vault.

They worked several more stores in the mall, including one liquor store that had shelves stripped bare. John checked it just in case something had been missed. He saw several 9mm pistol cartridge cases on the floor by a door leading to the back room. He carefully opened the door.

John theorized that that the owner or clerk on duty had managed to defend the store room from the looters, but had left when the fallout started. Whatever actually had taken place; there were several cases of alcohol left intact. Most of the beer and wine had frozen and burst during the frigid winter. But the hard stuff had fared quite well.

John loaded up all the liquor and what beer and wine was still intact. He wasn't sure if the beer and wine would still be good, even if the containers hadn't burst, but he would take it and test it later.

Their five hours were about up when John saw the three-golden ball sign of a pawn shop. It was locked up tight, with all the security shutters intact, though the windows were broken out. "This could be a good haul," he told Belinda. "You willing to risk a little more time here?"

"If you think it worth it," Belinda replied.

Working quickly John fired up another thermal lance and had the door security gate out of the way in short order, and then the triple locks of the door itself. When he entered, he whistled. It didn't look like anything had been touched.

There were a few guns hanging here and there, but John checked the back room first. It was a mother lode. John and Belinda began to load up the truck, first with guns, and then tools of every type. They skipped over the electronics for the most part. Though they had taken prime pieces of jewelry from some of the other places they'd hit, John had Belinda throw everything in the display cases into boxes. They'd sort the good from the bad later.

The pickup was overflowing when they stopped, and their dosimeters were showing 28R of accumulated radiation. John wasted no time getting out of the high radiation zone. Again, they headed back to the Farm without stopping to overnight in the open again.

John decided they'd been very lucky. He wouldn't cut things so fine in the future. The snow started the morning after they got to the Farm, and didn't stop for six days. No one left or entered the Farm for over a month. He and Belinda both showed signs of mild radiation poisoning, but the symptoms faded. Only time would tell if their continued dosages would result in early cancers or other medical effects.

John and Belinda had plenty of free time during that winter to sort and catalog their scavenging haul. With the number of people now living at the Farm, each only worked two days a week at the jobs they normally did, though John often did roaming security patrols on his own out around the Farm.

It was the worst winter yet. The several greenhouses that the Farm boasted really proved their worth. Tulsa had a lot of businesses that supported the oil fields of Oklahoma and Texas. John had managed to find several large single-phase diesel powered generator sets, so they were able to run the grow lights in the greenhouses much more than they had the previous winters.

It was coming up on April, and the snow was beginning to melt away, when Adam went to John's trailer to get him. "John," Adam said his face somber, "The Sinclair's place was hit last night. Judy was killed and Tom wounded. We don't know how bad. We just got the radio call a few minutes ago."

"I'll saddle up. One of the doctors going with me?"

"Yeah, Hillary. Arthur is still down with a cold."

"Who else?" John asked, leading the way out of the motorhome.

"Sandy Johnson and Jorge Martinez. They both have worked at the Sinclair place and know them well. Belinda is getting them started. They'll take the Ford one ton."

"She telling them to come armed?"

"Yes."

"Okay. I'll get the truck warmed up and pick up Hillary in a few minutes."

Adam hurried back to the main house to help his mother-in-law get her medical case ready for the trip.

It was less than two hours later that John was pulling into the front yard of Tom and Judy's small farm house. There was an obvious set of tracks in the snow going to the house, and another leading off in another direction from the house, plus a set to and from the barn.

John had Hillary wait in the truck while he, Sandy, and Jorge checked around the place. When they couldn't find anyone about outside, John entered the house. He came back to the door a few moments later and motioned to Hillary. Sandy ran over to John's truck and carried her medical bag for her as she worked her way to the house through the deep snow.

While Hillary tended to Tom's injuries, John asked him, "What happened?"

"That bucket of slime knocked on the door yesterday evening, begging for food. You know we don't have much, but Judy, bless her soul, insisted we let him in so she could feed him. He didn't have any obvious gun, but I still didn't trust him. I had to argue with Judy to not let him stay in the house. Did let him stay in the barn.

"Well, this morning Judy was up getting the tea started when that low-life busted in the front door and demanded more food. He was carrying an AR-15 of some kind. You know Judy. Kindest woman you'd ever want to meet. But very protective of the place. She threw the hot water she had ready for tea in his face and he shot her.

"I heard the commotion and came out with my Colt .45 and he shot me a couple of times. I guess I went down and passed out. He was gone when I came to, and so was my Colt .45 and all the food that could be carried easily."

Tom groaned in pain suddenly and slumped back. He managed to rise up a little and lift one hand to put on John's chest. "You got to get him for what he done to Judy. I ain't going to be able to do it. You find him, you can't miss him. He totally bald headed and kinda puny looking."

He slumped back, passing out again, and Hillary said, "That's enough, John. Let me work on him in peace. I need to get him stabilized before we take him to the Farm."

"Okay," John replied. He turned to Sandy and Jorge, who were standing in the doorway. "Check the animals and take care of them. Keep an eye out."

John helped where he could as Hillary attended to Tom. When she'd done all she could, John called Sandy and Jorge in to carry Tom out to the Ford. It was a crew cab model and had a bench type second seat. They put Tom on the seat and loosely strapped him in with the seatbelts.

Hillary rode with Sandy, to keep an eye on Tom, and Jorge rode back with John. Hillary and June went to work on Tom again as soon as they had him in the room set aside as an infirmary.

John filled Adam in on what Tom had told him. "We're going back to get Judy's body, and I'm going after this guy."

"Maybe you should wait for better weather," Adam suggested, knowing John wouldn't.

"It's better with the snow still on the ground. I should be able to track him easily. He must have been really desperate. He hasn't made a mistake like this before."

"You think it's the leader of that gang?"

"Yes, I do. The captives said he was bald and scrawny. I think he probably got a big dose of radiation, just not enough to kill him."

"At least take someone with you," Adam said.

John was shaking his head. "I can travel faster and more easily by myself. I'm going to go get ready. Have Sandy and Jorge wait here for me."

There was a small group of people waiting outside the main Farm house when John exited. John saw Belinda but didn't stop to talk to her. She'd probably try to talk him out of going, or at least take her along.

Belinda watched John walk by without acknowledging her, and then turned to ask Adam what was going on. But Adam was already back in the house. Belinda knew she would find out what was going on, but decided not to try to find out from John. He seemed bent on a mission. Adam or June would tell her what was going on in their own time.

John climbed onto the rear seat of the Ford, when he returned wearing one of his Kifaru packs. He had the HK-91 slung over his shoulder, along with his musette bag of magazines. He also wore the Para-Ordinance P-14 on his hip.

When Sandy drove up to Tom's house again, John got out immediately. "Take care of Judy. I'll see you guys later."

Both men waved acknowledgment. They didn't really have time to say anything. John was already at the edge of the woods, striding out strongly in the tracks left by the bandit.

The man had a four-hour head start on John, and John figured he would be moving as fast as he could. After an hour of trudging along, John's heart fell slightly when he saw the new tracks in front of him. The man was on a quad of some kind. John listened, but didn't hear anything.

He debated about going back for one of the snowmobiles they'd scavenged, but decided against it. It would be better to take longer, but maintain the quietness of foot travel. The man would hear him coming hundreds of yards away on a snowmobile.

Resolutely John headed after the quad and the man riding it. He walked all day, following the tracks. He saw where the man had stopped to urinate. It was difficult to tell how far ahead the man might be, but the tracks of the quad were fairly sharp and clear.

John traveled until almost dark. It was too dangerous to continue in the dark, even with the night vision goggles. He set up camp, had a hot supper, and went to bed, confident the perimeter alarms would warn him if the man chanced to double back in the dark.

He was up early the next morning, well before daylight. The sky was showing only a little light when he started following the tracks again. John was surprised that he didn't find any sign of a camp after he'd traveled at least three miles. The tracks were looking different. John decided the man had continued through the night.

LOW PROFILE

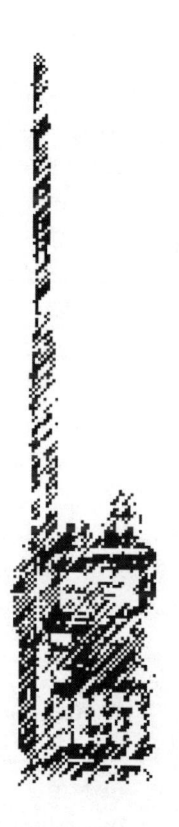

YAESU HANDHELD RADIO

John decided there was nothing else to do but continue following the tracks, so he trudged onward. It was late in the afternoon when John came up on the house. At the first sight of it, he stopped and crouched down, watching the house. An attempt to hide the quad had been made. It looked like a sheet had been thrown over it. But it hadn't been fastened well and was flapping in the slight breeze, drawing the eye.

After circling the house carefully, John decided the man was in the house. But was he alone or were there more? And if so, were they with him, or his captives.

John cached the pack, and HK-91 in hand, began to approach the side of the house in a crouch. He got to the house apparently without being seen, and began edging along the side toward the front porch.

With still no sign of having been seen, John eased up onto the porch and over to the door. He debated for a moment what to do, realizing even as he was, that he should have made the decision before he got to this point. But a plan came to him and he edged past the door. He then reached over and knocked on it with his knuckles. "Hey! Anyone in there?"

John was glad he had moved to one side of the door. A burst of automatic fire splintered it. And then another burst finished knocking a large hole in the door. John had moved further away from the door and was at the edge of the window. He chanced a quick look into the room. John found himself looking into the face of Bobby Jones.

Bobby saw the motion at the window and turned his full auto M4 clone toward it. But he'd emptied the magazine in the two long bursts he'd fired. As he was trying to change magazines, John kicked in the window and stepped inside, the HK-91 muzzle aimed at Bobby's chest.

"Hey man! Don't shoot! I didn't know it was you!" He lifted his hands, but the M4 pistol grip was still in his right hand.

"Put it down, Bobby. Slow."

Bobby did, his eyes on John. "Come on man! Put down your gun. I said I didn't know it was you."

"Bobby, you've been going around robbing and killing people ever since the war! What's with you?"

LOW PROFILE

Bobby's look hardened. "Hey, man! A guy's got to live. You and your survivalist buddies can't keep everything to yourselves! It ain't fair, man!"

"Turn around," John said, making a small motion with the HK-91. John thought he was doing to do it, but Bobby lunged for the M4. John stepped forward and laid the butt of the rifle across the back of Bobby's neck, knocking him cold.

John keyed his Yaesu VX-7RB Amateur handheld that he used for medium range communications with the farm and reported what had happened. He quickly ran out to retrieve his pack to get some 550 cord to tie up Bobby before he came to.

When Bobby did come to somewhat later, with a loud groan, he was sitting propped up on the sofa, his hands tied behind his back, and his feet tied together. "I'll get you for this!" he growled at John, who was sitting in a chair facing the sofa.

"Don't make it any worse," John said quietly. "Tell me why you did all this."

"Screw you!" was the only reply. At least for a little while.

"You think you had me fooled, don't you? That I didn't know what you were doing. Well, I'll tell you this, when you sold your house I got a look inside. You had a fallout shelter all that time and didn't tell me. Man, that was lame! I was your best friend! Took you shooting. Let you help me with the Jeep. And you went and held out on me.

"But I got to use that shelter. The goofs that bought the place didn't even know what hit them." Bobby's face changed slightly. "But I couldn't get in until they finally came out. Look at me! It's all your fault I got radiation sickness! If I'd known where your new house was... Things would have been different." He was glaring at John.

"So you decided you could just take what you wanted at the point of a gun?"

"I told you before the war that I would. It's the only way. I ain't going to labor on no farm for hours just for a bowl of soup. How do you think I felt when I found out you were a big cheese at that farm? Huh? You should have included me! But no, you just helped your farm friends. I had to take care of myself."

"We helped lots of people, Bobby. I would have helped you if you'd come to me."

"I wasn't going to crawl on my belly to you. I told you I don't do farm work."

John saw a glimpse of fear in Bobby's eyes when the sound of the Ford crew cab came through the mutilated door and window.

"What's going on," Bobby asked.

"We're taking you back to the Farm to stand trial," John replied.

"You got no right! It's every man for himself. I only did what I had to!"

"Save it for the jury, Bobby."

Bobby continued to protest as Sandy and Jorge carried him out to the Ford and put him on the back seat. John climbed in beside him, after putting his pack and rifle in the bed of the truck.

"What about the quad?" Jorge asked.

"We'll come back for it. I want to get him squared away at the Farm first."

Sandy and Jorge got back into the truck and they headed for the farm. Again, one of the empty storage rooms was used as a holding cell. John untied Bobby and gave him a slight shove to get him into the room before he could try anything. Bobby was still screaming obscenities when John left the storage barn.

John saw Belinda with a group of people that had been watching what went on. He called out to her. "I need someone to go with me to bring back his stuff. You want to come?"

Belinda nodded. "Just give me a minute." She was wearing her pistol and whippet, but Belinda ran to her trailer to retrieve the AUG and accoutrements. She met him at his truck. Jorge was there as well.

"Jorge is going to bring the quad back," John said as Jorge climbed into the bed of the truck and made himself comfortable. Belinda climbed into the passenger seat of the truck and John got in the other side.

John and Jorge checked the fuel level in the quad. It was almost empty. They looked around and found several empty fuel cans, and one partially full of gasoline. Jorge used it to fill the quad. They put the empty cans in the back of John's truck. Jorge headed back toward the Farm as fast as the quad would go, considering the road conditions.

Belinda kept watch while John searched the rest of the small farm. There were signs that Bobby had killed at least one person in the house sometime in the past, but John found no body. The house was in poor shape, trash everywhere. He found some loaded magazines for Bobby's M4. He gathered them up with the carbine and carried them out to the truck. He couldn't find any other ammunition. There was no food left, either. Bobby had apparently eaten everything he'd taken from Tom's place.

When he got to the barn, he was surprised to find Bobby's Jeep intact. He checked it for fuel. It was full. He'd found a set of keys in the living room of the house and tried the one he thought would work. It did. The Jeep started up, but ran rather roughly. It smoothed out some after it had warmed up, but John decided the gasoline was probably well past its prime.

John opened up the barn doors and backed the Jeep out and moved it over beside the pickup. "Bobby's pride and joy," John told Belinda when she walked over to look at it.

"I want to look around in the barn a little more. See if it looks like he stashed anything," John said, walking back to the barn as Belinda moved back to take a look around the place, just in case.

John couldn't find anything else that didn't seem to belong there, so he went back outside. "Belinda, if you'll drive my truck, I'll take the Jeep to the Farm." Belinda nodded and the two set off.

With the weather still rather marginal, and supplies strained from the long harsh winter, none of the other groups around the area were willing to send representatives to the Farm for another trial.

John suspected that there was some general reluctance, as well. Trials and executions weren't that big of a draw, once the newness was off. And it worn off in a big way during the first trial and set of executions.

Adam, June, and several of the others at the Farm that helped Adam make decisions came to the conclusion to keep Bobby prisoner until later in the spring when people would be moving about to start trading again. It was against John's advice. He wanted the trial and sentencing done now, by those on the Farm. But he took the decision in stride.

John made sure Bobby was secure, checking the storage room every day. He would have preferred a guard be kept 24/7, but he was overruled on that issue, as well. Everyone that was suitable to be a guard was needed in the fields, barns, and greenhouses.

The snow was gone, and the date of the trial set for late June. John was anxious to get back to the railroad yard and port at Tulsa to try to recover whatever they could find. But he didn't want to be gone during the trial. So he chaffed a bit at the waiting.

LOW PROFILE

It was well he waited, for one of the former captives of the gang was a turncoat and had been giving Bobby information gleaned from the other captives while they had been with the gang. On a particularly busy day, Karen Clemson went to the storage barn and released Bobby.

She had his weapons and his keys for the Jeep with her. They were in the Jeep by the time anyone saw them and raised the alarm. They had been gone for almost ten minutes when John got to his truck.

John didn't hesitate. He grabbed his rifle and took off after the Jeep in his truck, alone.

There weren't many places Bobby could go. John was sure he was headed for Tulsa, to lose himself in remains of the city, so he followed the shortest route to the city himself. Sure enough, after an hour of driving as fast as he could with the conditions what they were, John caught sight of the Jeep ahead of him. It was still barreling along at the highest speed Bobby could get it to.

John didn't think Bobby saw him slowly closing the distance for quite some time. But apparently, he did. The Jeep swerved a little, and then picked up a fraction more speed. John was a half a mile behind, still barely gaining on the Jeep.

John had approached within a quarter of a mile when Bobby suddenly turned off the main road. John couldn't feature why, at first, but then he got an idea. Bobby was heading for Crunch Hill, to get away from John. Bobby knew a truck like John's couldn't climb it.

"You've got to be kidding," John said aloud. But that was exactly what Bobby had in mind. They were approaching the point where the rock climbers turned up the hill for their challenges. John saw the Jeep suddenly come to a sliding stop. There was the sound of a shot and Karen fell out of the passenger side of the Jeep.

Bobby headed up the slope bouncing over rocks, going faster than he probably ever had before. The pickup slid to a stop and John jumped out to check Karen. She was dead. Bobby was a hundred yards up the slope and to John's amazement the Jeep stopped and Bobby appeared beside it, his M4 in hand. John dove for cover when Bobby dumped the rest of the thirty-round magazine at him, full auto. It was only the one long burst and Bobby was back in the Jeep, headed upward again.

John had no clue where the rounds had gone, but none had hit him, or come close. He jumped for the pickup again and tore up the road, wondering if Bobby was actually this dumb, or if he had some kind of plan John couldn't figure out.

The rear of the truck sliding on the dirt track, John took the long way around to the top of the hill. He didn't clear the top of the hill. He stopped, grabbed the HK-91, and ran the rest of the way.

There was Bobby; thirty yards away, still climbing the rocky hill. All of Bobby's attention was on the path he was taking up the hill. He never even saw John until he made the top and started to look around to see if John was going to actually try to climb up behind him.

When he turned, it took a fraction of a second to realize John was standing right there, twenty feet away, the HK-91 lined up on him.

"How…" was all he had time to say before the 150-grain soft point bullet bored through his forehead and out the back of his skull.

Walking over to the body slumped in the driver's seat of the Jeep, John whispered, "Why, Bobby? Why?" He didn't get an answer.

It took the rest of the day to get the bodies and Jeep back to the Farm. Bobby and Karen were buried in a common grave the next day.

LOW PROFILE

CHAPTER NINE

With the spring planting done, John and his scavenging crew headed once more to Tulsa. Things turned out quite a bit different than they were expecting. There had been some chatter on the Amateur Bands of the Federal and State governments operating again, in some locations.

John hadn't heard anything about Tulsa being one of the cities that had National Guard and Regular Military enforcing martial law, so it came as a great surprise when John suddenly had to stop the pickup when they went around a curve just outside of Tulsa.

The three semi-trucks behind John all came to a halt as well. "Let's take it real easy," John quietly told Belinda. "Tell the others."

John got out of the pickup slowly, as Belinda keyed the FRS radio and told the others what John had said.

"What's up?" John asked, carefully keeping his hands spread away from his body slightly.

The Lieutenant that was walking up from behind the two vehicles blocking the road spoke. The two PFC's, both with M4's at the ready coming with him said nothing.

"Tulsa is now under martial law. State your business," the Lieutenant said. "And what are you carrying in the trucks?"

"We were going in to Tulsa to look for supplies," John said, choosing his words carefully. "The trucks are empty. You're more than free to check."

"We will," the Lieutenant replied motioning for the two PFC's to do just that.

"All clear," came the call a few minutes later when each of the three trailers had been opened and checked.

"I'm afraid that all remaining equipment and supplies in Tulsa and immediate surrounding area are delegated for the military and the residents of Tulsa. Turn around and go back the way you come," the Lieutenant said. "I would advise you to let people in your area know that the days of indiscriminate looting are over. It would be advisable that you stay within twenty-five miles of your homes."

John nodded. "We'll pass the word. Is this going on all over?"

"I don't have that information," said the Lieutenant. "But the President has mandated that a recovery process will proceed, to bring the United States back to its previous status as a world power."

John nodded again. A thought occurred to him and he asked, "Are there ways and means to get travel permits?"

The Lieutenant was silent for several long moments. "It is possible, but not recommended. You can contact headquarters in Tulsa by radio for more information." The Lieutenant gave John an Amateur Radio frequency. "That frequency is monitored for contact with outlying communities. You are free to pass it along, too."

John nodded one last time and directed the semis to get turned around and head back to the Farm. He turned the pickup around and followed the semis. As soon as they got back to the Farm, John located Adam and they sat down in the main house for John to tell Adam what had happened and discuss the matter.

"Apparently, they aren't confiscating firearms yet, since they didn't take yours," Adam said. "Do you think they are confiscating food?"

"They didn't mention it," John replied. "I think it will be a good idea to get on their good side. It was obvious that we were out to scavenge, though they used the term looting. It might be a good idea to offer them what fresh food and biodiesel we can spare and still take care of the Farm and the groups we're supporting."

"Just give it to them?" Adam asked. He sounded reluctant.

"If need be. There is a chance they'll offer some type of scrip for redemption later. I doubt seriously they'll trade for it or use gold and silver. It will be common knowledge very soon that we are doing well here. I'd rather head off attempts to take what we have, by voluntarily offering our help for the rebuilding."

"We'd better talk this over with some of the others. They have a stake in what goes on."

John nodded. "To my way of thinking, the final decision is yours, though."

Adam called for the equivalent of a town meeting for the next evening. All the equipment was moved out of the equipment barn and they met there. Adam lined out the situation as he and John had discussed.

There were more than a few dissenters against the plan to volunteer supplies to the military, much to Adam's dismay.

John, standing out in the crowd with the others, spoke up. "I think it is in our best interests to help get the country back on its feet. There haven't been any indications yet that the military will use strong arm tactics. If that happens… that is another discussion."

"I, for one, intend to cooperate with the authorities until and unless they prove themselves our enemy, rather than our friend."

There was quite a bit of angry muttering about John's statements.

"We don't even know who the president is!" someone protested.

Adam quickly said, "We'll find out. We'll find out quite a bit more before we make a decision. That's all for tonight."

Adam looked somber when everyone had dispersed and it was just him and John left in the barn. "John..." Adam started to say.

"I'm sorry it came out the way it did," John said, interrupting Adam. "But it is what I feel. I'll be the first one on the firing line if it turns out the military goes fascist on us. But cooperation that doesn't violate my personal principles is what I intend to do. I'm just one person. It won't affect the Farm very much, no matter what I do."

"You're looked up to by many of those here. And you've been a solid support for me," Adam replied slowly. "I don't want to lose that. But I have responsibilities here that I can't shirk."

"I know. I don't mean to put you on a spot, but I have to go with my beliefs."

Adam nodded. "Of course. And that is what I'll do, too."

"A decision, if it is to cooperate, needs to be made in a day or two. I don't think it'll make much difference when the decision is announced if it is to stand firm on our own."

"Yeah. I'll decide by day after tomorrow."

They left it at that and split up, Adam going to the main house and John to his motorhome.

John spent the rest of the day in his storage room the next day after he'd put in his time in the greenhouses, harvesting the current crop of fresh food. He had a pretty good handle on what he had in storage, but he wanted to update his computer files.

He lost track of time and was late getting to supper at the main house. Adam and the others looked at him questioningly. "Sorry," he said, blushing slightly. "I was doing inventory and lost track of the time."

There was little conversation at the table that evening. Everyone seemed lost in their own thoughts. Adam looked a little pale. John could tell that the decision was weighing on him. It wasn't as clear cut to Adam as it was to John, and John knew and understood that. John could leave whenever he wanted. Adam had responsibilities at the Farm. The decision would affect him greatly. Not so John.

The next morning Adam was knocking on John's motorhome door at five. When John opened the door it didn't look like Adam had been to bed the previous night.

"John. I need to talk to you."

"Come on in," John said. He started a pot of coffee while Adam sat down at the dinette.

"I've been trying to make that decision all night," Adam said, his hands one on top of the other on the dinette table. John stayed quiet and let Adam proceed at his own pace.

"I'm inclined to agree with you that we should be a force to help the country recover rather than just taking care of ourselves… That's kind of what we have done here, you know."

John nodded and Adam continued. "But I have to tell you, I'm not inclined to take on the responsibility of dealing with it. If you're willing to be the Farm's… Ambassador, I guess… to the Military, I'm prepared to follow your suggestions."

"Representative, perhaps," John said with a chuckle. "Ambassador is a little highfalutin. I guess, to get things set up, I could do that. You know I much prefer to keep a much lower profile than that."

Adam was smiling in relief. "Well, I think you can handle it for a while."

They sat and drank coffee for a little while, discussing some of the particulars that John would be talking to the military authorities about.

John made contact that afternoon and set up a meeting in Tulsa with the commander of the local military detachment for the following day. He spent most of the evening typing up a proposal based on his discussion with Adam. With five copies printed out, John headed for Tulsa the following morning.

The team at the roadblock was expecting him and one of the soldiers gave him directions into town. John had his HK-91 with him, but left it in the truck when he got to the headquarters building and exited the truck. He did have his P-14 holstered. No one said anything about it when he was shown in to the commanding officer of the Tulsa detachment.

Colonel Thaddeus Andrews looked rather grim when John was presented to him. "I don't have much time. What exactly is it you are here to do?" He motioned to a chair in front of the Colonel's desk and John sat down.

"Colonel, I'm representing a group of farm people northwest of town. We have managed to survive and... while I won't say we are flourishing we have been able to contribute significantly to the survival of several other groups and individuals in the area.

"We look forward to the time when things return to a somewhat more normal status. We would like to contribute to achieving that end. Though we don't have a great deal of excess production, we do have enough to contribute fresh foods to your command. We also produce enough biodiesel to provide a hundred gallons every two weeks. I know it isn't much, but that is all the extra we have, even being as conservative as we are." He handed the Colonel the copies of the proposal. The Colonel didn't look at it.

Colonel Andrews studied John for several long moments, and then finally said, "We have the authority to requisition anything we need, without explanation or compensation."

"I thought that might be the case," John said evenly. "And I don't think most of those at the Farm would attempt to fight against it."

"I take it you would."

John smiled slightly. "Oh, I'd never do that."

"Of course," Colonel Andrews replied dryly. "If I was to take you up on your offer, what's in it for your farm?"

"Actually, it is my friends' farm. I just work there for room and board and found. His name is Adam and his wife's name is June. Markum. June's parents are the local medical system, along with June, who is a nurse. But they are both up there in years and we will eventually be without good medical care.

"We're hoping we will be able to obtain such care from the military until we can find other doctors. Of course, best case, is we would get paid for what we provide, and have the medical care."

"Not asking for a lot, are you?"

"Not really," John said, "In my opinion."

"I can assure you, you won't be paid for the products. At least not in gold or silver. And I doubt you'd take the old dollars. Scrip, for future recompense is a possibility. I will send this offer of yours up the line and get back to you."

John nodded and stood. The Colonel held out his right hand and John shook it earnestly. "I think this will be a mutually beneficial arrangement."

"Don't count your chickens before the eggs hatch. We will always reserve the right to take what we need. For the good of the entire country."

"Yes. Of course." John left the office and the Colonel called for the Lieutenant sitting at the desk in the outer office.

When John left, he drove to his place in the gated community. The gates stood open, but when he drove around, John didn't see anyone about. A quick look at the entry to his basement home didn't indicate any attempts to breach it. He headed back to the Farm.

John didn't expect any response for a few days. Therefore, he was surprised when, after two days had passed, a Blackhawk helicopter showed up mid-morning and circled the Farm area several times.

After the third pass over the main Farm house, the Blackhawk began to land in the big pasture behind the animal barn, scattering the stock to the far reaches of the pasture. When John and Adam showed up a few minutes later, there were nearly a dozen people near the barn, all armed.

John went through the gate and headed for the helicopter a few yards away. He'd barely started when three men climbed out of the Blackhawk. John immediately recognized one of them as Colonel Andrews.

"Colonel Andrews," John said, his voice raised to be heard over the sound of the helicopter. But the pilot killed the engine and things began quieting.

"Mr. Havingsworth," replied the Colonel, taking John's outstretched hand. "Is there somewhere where we can talk? With you and Mr. Markum, I think it was."

"Of course. Up at the main house. This way, please." John guided the three officers toward the gate of the pasture.

"You seem quite prepared to handle trouble," the Colonel said conversationally as they passed the group of armed Farm personnel.

"We are. Colonel, this is Adam Markum, the owner of this ranch, with his wife."

"Colonel," Adam said, holding out his hand.

The Colonel shook Adam's hand, replying, "Mr. Markum."

The other two officers remained quiet as they followed along, headed for the main house. One was a man, the other a woman. The man was a Lieutenant, the woman a Captain. They looked around curiously as Adam, John, and the Colonel walked ahead of them.

When June had them settled in the dining room of the house, the Colonel introduced the other two officers. "This is Lieutenant Harold Randolph and Captain Rebecca Hood. The Lieutenant is in charge of local procurement, and Captain Hood is head of the medical detachment in Tulsa."

After greetings all around, the three officers sat down, as did John, Adam, and June. Belinda was hovering by the door. "Would you care for coffee?" June asked the officers.

All three looked surprised. "You still have coffee?" Lieutenant Randolph asked.

"A small quantity. It's only for special occasions, now," June replied as Belinda scurried off to get the coffee ready for them.

The Colonel didn't wait for the coffee. He got right down to business.

"I've spoken to General Braddock," Colonel Andrews said. "He is inclined to accept your offer. However, he has left it up to me to make the final decision. And submit a report on why I made the decision I intend to make today. The proposal submitted was informative. I need a few more details."

"Anything you need," Adam said after glancing at John, who said nothing, "you just have to ask."

"Can you," Colonel Andrews asked June, "or your parents, I believe, go over your medical capabilities with Captain Hood? Lt. Randolph and I would like to look over the operation a bit more closely than we could from the air."

"Certainly," Adam said and he and June both rose. The three officers rose as well. "Aren't you coming?" Adam asked John.

John shook his head. "No. You can explain much better than I." He grinned. "I just work here. But I will be around if you need me."

The group split up, cups of coffee in hand, and John headed back to his motorhome. He enjoyed the coffee and made a mental note to remember to take the cup back. John thought about the future, and possibilities, now that things were changing.

Nearly three hours later Adam called John on his FRS radio, and John headed back up to the house. He saw the indecision on the Colonel's face when June asked them to stay for lunch. It was ready, and there was enough for all, including the helo crew.

"Very well," Colonel Andrews replied.

The meeting was scheduled for after the meal. No discussion of it would take place during the lunch. After serving the table, Belinda and Serena carried portions out to the helicopter. The three officers didn't seem to want to talk, anyway. They were enjoying the fresh food too much.

After the meal, with another cup of coffee each, Adam asked, "And have you made a decision, Colonel?"

"Other than some details, yes, I have. The Tulsa operation will take you up on your offer. You will get signed receipts for everything you provide to us. You will be able collect at some time in the future, when a new currency is designed and printed."

John managed to keep his face expressionless. Adam less so. He had a slightly sick look on his face.

"I assure you," Colonel Andrews said slowly, "That the receipts will, in time, be worth something."

Adam nodded. "Yes, sir. We'll hold up our end of the bargain. In the quantities we discussed."

"That is all I ask," replied Colonel Andrews replied, standing. Adam took his hand and shook it when the Colonel offered it.

"Thank you, Colonel, Captain, Lieutenant," John said, shaking each one's hand in turn. All were silent as they went back out to the helicopter. When the pilot saw them coming, she began the startup process. The rotors were whirling when they arrived. John stopped outside the rotor's wash and watched the three officers enter the helicopter. Moments later the Blackhawk was lifting off, turning toward Tulsa as it did so.

With Adam's authority to negotiate for the Farm, John went to Tulsa two days later with the first bob truck load of food for the military outpost. John met with Lt. Randolph and got detailed receipts signed for everything John delivered that day. As soon as John got back to the Farm, he and Adam copied everything and put the originals in Adam's fire resistant filing cabinet, with the copy going to John for storage in a fire-resistant document case he had in the motorhome.

The first few weeks John went in with every shipment until the process was routine. He took along Adam's long time Farm manager, Cletus Du'bois, getting him comfortable with the process, ostensibly as a backup, much to Cletus' dismay. Cletus would be doing the work on his own, soon, though John had not said that outright. Adam had his suspicions, but said nothing until John brought up the subject.

It was July 4, during the simple celebration the Farm was holding, when John took Adam aside for a private talk. "Adam," John said, "I'm getting ready to head out for a while. The Farm is going well, and the military has lived up to its agreement. You may or may not ever see a return on the receipts, but the chance of bandits is pretty much gone. You're assured of decent medical care, even if Hillary and Arthur do retire, the way they've been talking."

"I had a feeling this was coming," Adam admitted. "Can't say I was looking forward to it. But I won't try to talk you out of it. You've helped us get where we are, and I have to agree. We are in as good of shape as anyone could ask for after nuclear war."

"There is one other factor," John said. "Belinda had people in Missouri, not far from my place. She talks about trying to get back there sometime to see if they are alive. She hasn't been able to get any word through the Amateurs. I'm going to offer to take her there, and bring her back if no one is there. You have a say in that."

"I'm not about to tell anyone they can't leave!" Adam replied, a bit upset at his perception of what John was saying.

"Of course you wouldn't," John said hastily. "The question is more if she'd be welcome back if she does leave and then finds there is no one there with whom she can stay and have a life."

"Oh. Well, I can't think of any reason why she wouldn't be welcome back."

"We're still getting the occasional new resident," John reminded Adam.

"That's true," Adam said thoughtfully. But he shook his head and said, "But that doesn't matter. She's been an asset. We can hold her place for up to two years. No telling how long it will take to travel there and back, things being what they are."

"I'll tell her," John said. "She may not even want to go, as you said, things being what they are."

John asked Belinda the next day if she wanted to go, making it clear that there would be no strings attached if she did, in light of the fact that they spent a lot of time together and several of the matchmakers on the Farm were trying to get them to become a couple.

"Oh, yes! I would like to go. My parents weren't as prepared as Adam here, but I have to believe they might have made it. I would at least like to know, either way. I can't stop thinking about them."

"Okay, then. We'll leave in a week. We'll be taking a trailer, so you can bring anything you want. You might want to talk to Adam about your leaving."

"Of course. I owe him and June so much. I just hope they'll take me back if things don't work out."

"Oh, I'm sure of it," John said, a slight smile on his face.

It took more than a week to get the travel permits in order. Colonel Andrews seemed as annoyed as John at the delays. The various jurisdictions along the route John wanted to take each had their own requirements for travel into, through, and out of their territory. Almost two weeks after John's announcement that he was going on the trip and first requested the documents, Colonel Andrew's aide contacted the Farm and let John know he could pick up the documents whenever he wanted.

Belinda was as ready as John to get started. Her duties had ended the first week of the wait, and she'd been at loose ends since. The truck and trailer had been packed and repacked. John and Belinda were more than ready when John got the word. They left the Farm a few minutes after Adam came down to John's motorhome and told him.

They had to go into Tulsa to get the papers. There was an entire packet of them, divided in sections with paperclips. The Colonel's aide gave John the papers and he and Belinda turned to leave, but the Lieutenant said, "The Colonel would like to see you before you go."

"Of course," John replied, maintaining his patient demeanor.

After the aide called the Colonel on the intercom, he showed the two into Colonel Andrews' office.

"Have a seat," Colonel Andrews. "I know you must be in something in a hurry to get going, considering the delays. I won't take much of your time." Despite his words, Colonel Andrews paused and didn't say anything for several long moments.

Then the Colonel opened a drawer of his desk and took out a large manila envelope. "I didn't want you to think the travel papers were dependent on what I am about to ask you to do. That wouldn't be right, and it wouldn't be the truth." Again he paused, still holding the envelope.

"I have a personal favor to ask," he finally said.

"Of course, Colonel Andrews," John replied.

"I have family near the route your taking. I was hoping you would deliver this to them." The Colonel handed the envelope to John.

John was a bit surprised how heavy the envelope was. The Colonel saw the surprise in John's eyes. "It's best you know what is in it, I suppose," he said. "It's mostly just a few letters I've written to my family since the war. And there is some gold I've saved in there for them. I just have to trust you to deliver it intact, if you do agree to. The letters are more important to me than the gold, but if it is like everywhere else, they may be having a hard time and could use it."

"It will all get there, if any of it does. I can't guarantee it, since I can't guarantee we'll make it. It's still a rough world out there."

"I understand that. And I would like to make it worth your while trying. I have a bit more gold and some silver, but I have no idea what to offer you."

"Post is important. I'll know it is a real sign things are coming back when there is regular service. But it has to be practical. What would you say to a silver dime for delivery?"

Colonel Andrews looked incredulous. "Just a single dime? Are you kidding?"

John shook his head. "That is a high price to many people around here. I'm not out to gouge you."

"Well… I don't know what to say," the Colonel said.

"That is in advance," John said, smiling slightly, "success or failure."

Colonel Andrews laughed. "Of course." He opened a different desk drawer and took out a pre-1965 silver dime and handed it to John. It was so worn John couldn't read the date or the mint mark, but that was all right. It was obviously a silver dime.

John and Belinda took their leave, and the trip was on.

CHAPTER TEN

John had allowed plenty of time for the trip, despite how easy it should be. They would be traveling along I-44 all the way, with a couple of short side trips. Most of the travel would be in the various military jurisdictions, but the jurisdictions didn't all meet edge to edge. There were still some areas without the benefit of military presence.

The reports were, including those passed along by the military, and others by Amateur Radio Operators, that these open zones could still be dangerous for travelers. Between that and the fact that travel restrictions were in place, there would not be many travelers on the road. John and Belinda would more or less be on their own for much of the trip.

There weren't going to be motels, restaurants, and filling stations open along the route. But John was confident he had enough fuel and supplies to make a round trip, with enough extra of everything for unforeseen events, and for trading along the way.

The first few miles of the trip east on I-44 from Tulsa weren't too bad. There had been a lot of scavenging done by those survivors east and north of Tulsa. The Military had also done some salvage and cleanup work up to thirty miles out from Tulsa.

John showed the sentries at the blockade at the furthest point of the Tulsa Military Administrative Zone his and Belinda's travel documents. There was no problem with them passing.

After clearing the road block, on general principles, John stopped whenever he saw anything that might be useful, or hold something useful. There wasn't much to be found. Only a few miles beyond the blockade, there were signs of intensive scavenging. John thought it was probably an organized group, probably from as far away as Joplin, Missouri. The Farm was in contact with an Amateur there. He had not said the city was sending teams out, but there were hints here and there of the fact.

John and Belinda fell into their standard travel routine of having a hot breakfast, cold lunch, and an early hot supper, after which they would travel a bit more before setting up camp out of sight of the Interstate. Each had their own tent and shared the privacy tents for the chemical toilet and the solar heated shower bag. Whenever they ran across a water supply, John stopped and they filled their water containers, using John's Katadyn Expedition filter.

At each stop John got out his Brunton ADC Pro pocket weather instrument and checked current conditions. The new weather pattern, along with being cooler in general, was also highly unpredictable. Watching the clouds and tracking the winds and barometric pressure gave John enough information to have a decent idea of probable local short term conditions.

The colder climate meant drier summers, but did not mean no rain. Rain, when it came was usually in the form of a severe thunderstorm. During those, to conserve supplies, John and Belinda usually spent the daytime hours in John's Mountain Hardwear Trango 3.1 tent. It was larger than the small Eureka two-person tent John was providing Belinda.

Belinda had brought along a small library and read most of the time during those lulls. John read as well, though his reading material was on rewritable CD's and DVD's. He kept his lap top batteries charged using the twelve-volt system of the truck. The AA and AAA batteries for other things were charged with Brunton Solarpak 4.4 solar panels with BattJack battery chargers. The few items requiring C or D batteries were supplied with battery adapters that took AA batteries.

The first three days of the trip were uneventful. They stopped in Vinita and Miami for a few minutes each. Both had roadblocks at their exits from I-44. The people weren't aggressive, and would have let John and Belinda into their towns to do some trading if John and Belinda had been so inclined. Still having plenty of everything they needed, they passed on the opportunity and kept traveling each time.

The people manning the barricades at Vinita had good things to say about the people at Miami. They had cooperated on salvage operations until the Joplin people got involved. Those at Miami were equally appreciative of the Vinita residents. Neither had much good to say about Joplin. It hadn't been so bad until the Military made it presence known in Joplin.

Joplin was one of the locations whose Military command was requiring special travel papers for anyone going out of or coming into, the Joplin area. There was a roadblock at the state line between Oklahoma and Missouri.

From the looks of things, the Bradley IFV parked behind the barricade wasn't just for show. There were several vehicles along the edges of the road that showed the effects of the Bradley's 25mm chain gun.

John approached slowly, so as not to give those manning the Bradley any reason to open fire. A Sergeant stepped out from behind the blockade and approached the driver's side of the pickup. Two other men in uniform had rifles sighted on the truck from the edges of the blockade opening.

"Papers?" asked the Sergeant after John lowered his window.

"We're traveling through," John said, handing the man the appropriate set of transit papers.

"We'll be deciding that," replied the Sergeant negligently, as he carefully studied the papers. After several agonizing minutes for John and Belinda, the Sergeant looked at John again and said, "These look to be in order. Were you aware of the fuel toll?"

"Fuel toll?" John asked. "No."

"You either have to buy fuel or pay a tax on the fuel you have."

"We'll top off our tanks," John said carefully. "How much is it?"

"Is that fuel in the drums in the trailer?" the Sergeant asked.

"Some," John replied. "Water in some, too."

"How much fuel do you have?"

"Four drums of fuel. One empty drum of fuel, two full drums of fresh water," John replied, keeping his voice calm.

With a greedy smile on his face, the Sergeant then said, "Are you sure? If we find different, it all gets confiscated for attempted violation of martial law."

"I'm sure. You're free to check it."

"We'd check it whether we were free to, or not," replied the Sergeant. He went back to the trailer and stepped up on the running gear. He tapped each of the metal drums, and opened the two plastic ones.

"Well," he said, coming up to the cab of the truck again. "Seems to be as you said. The tax is a silver dime a gallon. Four fifty-five gallon drums. Two-hundred twenty gallons. Two hundred twenty silver dimes."

"We'll just fill up the other drum. How much is diesel?" John asked, getting the answer he expected.

"Four dimes a gallon. Two-hundred twenty dimes, plus a dime a gallon tax. Two-hundred seventy-five silver dimes total."

Looking eager then, the Sergeant asked, "You have gold?"

"Not much," John immediately responded.

"Only cost you two ounces of gold."

"I've only got one one-ounce Eagle and five tenth-ounce Eagles."

"Add a roll of dimes and you're out of here."

Though the Sergeant didn't notice, Belinda did, when John removed a gold one-ounce Eagle from one pocket of his shirt, the five tenth-ounce Eagles from the other pocket of his shirt, and the roll of dimes from the console of the truck.

John handed the Sergeant the precious metals. "Pull up past the Bradley. We'll fill that drum." When the drum was as full as it was going to get, the Sergeant said, "Stay on the Interstate. Do not go into Joplin. Understood?"

John nodded.

"The other side will be looking for you. You wind up late leaving, you could wind up dead."

"We won't be late," John replied, still calm as he could be.

Belinda couldn't believe his demeanor. He'd let them bribe him for passage past Joplin.

She couldn't stand it any longer after they had passed through the blockade on the south-east side of Joplin. "I can't believe you paid them a bribe!"

John smiled over at her. "I allowed for it. I have an agreement with the Colonel to report such actions to him when I get back. I'm supposed to get reimbursed."

"Oh. I didn't know," replied Belinda, looking chagrinned.

"I probably would have paid it, even if I wasn't going to get it back from the Colonel."

Belinda was startled at the look that crossed John's face momentarily. "I would be getting it back on my own, if not. With interest."

"I understand," Belinda said, feeling a shiver go down her back. John was serious.

Another day brought them near Springfield, Missouri. Like Tulsa, it had taken one of the small nukes. Also like Tulsa, it had a military presence, enforcing martial law. It was an honest command, like Tulsa, and unlike Joplin.

I-44 ran along the northern edge of Springfield. A five mile stretch of it was in the hot zone surrounding the crater. The sentries at the blockade on the west side of town gave them the option of going well around the hot zone, on side roads, or barreling through on the Interstate.

"How is the road?" John asked. "Still badly blocked?"

"You could probably make it in your rig," the Lieutenant said. With a grimace, he continued. "Too many people were out looting. They managed to clear a lane to get trucks and stuff through. Probably all died. Radiation in the hot spot is still 8R/hr."

John looked over at Belinda. "Could take us ten minutes or more through that zone, plus the time leading up to it when the radiation is also rising."

"We shouldn't pick up more than a 5 or 6R dose. I say we go the fast way," Belinda said after a moment's thought.

"Okay," John replied to Belinda, and then asked the Lieutenant, "You'll notify the blockade on the other side?"

The Lieutenant nodded.

LOW PROFILE

John drove carefully, but at speed, as they passed Springfield. Belinda had been just a bit high on her calculations. They only picked up a total of 4R additional radiation on the trip around Springfield.

They stopped outside of Northview to camp that night. Another storm was brewing and they set up for at least a two day stay.

They wound up staying four days, as the weather set in and didn't break. But break it finally did and they set off again. For the first time on the road, John had Belinda drive for a while, as he was nursing a summer cold and was feeling lousy. Belinda had made a large pot of hot lemonade and filled one of John's two-quart Stanley thermos so he could drink it on the way to help the congestion. In addition, John was sucking on peppermint candies to clear his sinuses and keep his throat moist.

As soon as he'd felt it coming on, two days before, he'd insisted on Belinda wearing a P-100 mask, and he did the same to prevent her from catching his illness. They continued to wear the masks, except when they were eating.

"Are you sure we shouldn't just set up camp again, until you're better," Belinda asked John as they approached Conway, Missouri.

John shook his head. "We can camp there overnight, but I want to keep traveling."

Though he was in the process of setting up his tent, Belinda left hers in its storage bag and helped John finish setting up his. As he stood helpless to counter her actions, she got his sleeping pad and sleeping bag arranged and ordered him to bed. He was too weak to resist.

Though they'd already stopped and eaten a hot meal of Mountain House rice and chicken, Belinda entered the tent and set up John's MSR multi-fuel stove in the alcove to heat up water to make him more hot lemonade. He didn't protest when Belinda insisted he take a dose of his stash of Nyquil to help him sleep after he'd downed another cup of the hot lemonade.

He was fast asleep when Belinda got her things and set them up on the other side of the tent from John. She wasn't going to leave him alone as sick as he was. She went back out and set up the rest of the camp, including the perimeter alarms.

Belinda took off her boots, but kept most of her clothes on when she laid down on top of her sleeping bag as the light was fading. She fell asleep sometime during the night. John's coughing woke her up the next morning. She helped him out to the privacy shelter for the chemical toilet, and then back to the tent. John was wearing a pair of boxer shorts and his back was clammy where she touched it to help him standup outside the tent.

"We're not traveling today," she said firmly, guiding him back to his tent. Much to her surprise, John was back in his sleeping bag when she went back in a few minutes later. She took her time preparing breakfast. She kept it simple. Oatmeal.

John ate listlessly, but he ate, knowing he needed to do so. He sat up, with the open sleeping bag around him, while he ate, and then drank half a cup of hot lemonade. He took another peppermint candy and lay back down.

When he didn't fall asleep shortly, Belinda persuaded him to take another shot of Nyquil, since they weren't going anywhere. He did so, grudgingly. When he was asleep, Belinda left the tent with her weapons and took another look around. They were in a good spot, and she wasn't too worried, but she wasn't going to take a chance.

Even she was getting antsy to change locations three days later when John insisted on it. He was past the worst of the cold, but still suffering some of the symptoms. Again Belinda drove. They didn't go far. Just to Lebanon. On a whim, Belinda asked the sentry at the city's blockade if the city happened to boast an open motel.

Very much to her surprise, the man said there was. Rather proudly, he added, "Got a restaurant, too. If you have precious metals, preferred, or something worthwhile to trade."

Considering herself on a roll, Belinda then asked about diesel fuel.

"Big Mike MacDougal makes biodiesel on his farm. He's selling it out of a tank truck at the old Chevron station."

"Thank you," Belinda said, thankful not only for what Lebanon had to offer, but that they were willing to offer it at all. It renewed her faith in people. Not everyone was like the military detachment at Joplin.

Belinda filled in John when she got back in the truck. He set his rifle aside and rested his head back on the headrest, his eyes closing. "I trust you. Wake me if you need me." He took a leather bag from inside of the console and handed it to her. Belinda looked inside. It was gold and silver.

They still had plenty of fuel, but John had said he planned to pick up fuel he was sure would be good on the way if he could. He was leery of petroleum diesel this long after the war that might be salvaged from trucks. Unless it was treated with PRI-D, he didn't want anything to do with it.

With that in mind, Belinda followed the directions the sentry had given to her to the Chevron station that was supposed to have the fuel. The sentry hadn't lied. Big Mike himself transferred the biodiesel from his tank truck to the drums in the trailer after they had decided on a price of one one-ounce Gold Eagle for the fuel. Big

Mike was happy with it. Belinda didn't think it was unreasonable.

Next she found the motel. The restaurant was adjacent to it and operated by the same people. John was still asleep in the truck when Belinda entered the motel office. "Hi," she said to the elderly woman sitting behind the check in counter. Belinda noted the shotgun leaning against the wall nearby.

The woman got up and stood behind the counter. Looking rather incredulous, the woman asked, "You traveling alone?"

Belinda shook her head. "No. He's in the truck."

"Oh. Good. It's not safe for a woman alone out there. Looking for a room, I take it."

Belinda nodded. "Depending on how much for the room and a couple of meals."

"Of course we are the only game in town." She smiled. "But I think we're reasonable. What do you have to trade?"

"We have some diesel, some feminine products, liquor, and tobacco. Also, some silver, if you prefer."

The woman's eyes lit up at the mention of the silver. "Meal is fifty cents silver, room five dollars in silver. Meal is mulligan stew, but the bathroom works and includes hot water for bath or shower. But the lights go out at ten."

Belinda hesitated a moment, but decided the rates really weren't unreasonable of travel accommodations nowadays. "Breakfast included?" Belinda asked.

This time the elderly woman hesitated. "I suppose. Be rice with honey and powdered milk."

"Good enough," Belinda replied. She turned away slightly as she opened the leather pouch. John kept his precious metals in plastic coin tubes. She counted out ten silver half dollars and four quarters. After a moment, she took out two silver dimes as well.

Belinda handed the silver coins to the woman and said, "The extra is for breakfast. I wasn't trying to put you on the spot."

"Why... Thank you," the woman said, gratefully. "Most try to knock the price down. We're just barely making it as it is. Not many travelers. Mostly military. We did okay when they were here, but they sure cleaned us out. But we have diesel to keep the gen running for several weeks now."

Belinda nodded and followed the woman out of the office. The woman had picked up the shotgun and carried it in one hand as she led Belinda to the nearest room. When Belinda saw the single king sized bed she paused. "Actually," she said then, "We need two beds."

"Oh. Okay," came the reply. "Next room has twin queens."

They moved to the next room down the line and the woman opened it with her pass key. "I'll bring the room keys back in a few minutes," she said, hurrying back to the office.

Belinda moved the truck and woke John up. He nodded in approval when he saw the room and Belinda told him there was hot water for a soaking bath. "Do you want to do that first or eat? They have a mulligan stew going."

"Let's get settled first, and then eat. I'll do a soak and hot toddy and then go to bed. You okay with setting things up again?"

"Of course," Belinda replied, headed for the door to get their packs. She met the woman coming back with the keys. Belinda took the keys and told the woman, "There'll be an alarm system around the truck. You might warn anyone else around the place to steer clear. We'll be in for supper in a little while."

The woman nodded and said, "Can't blame you for that. One of my boys takes a turn around the place from time to time during the night. Can't be too careful." She hurried back to the office.

They both used the bathroom and then went to the small restaurant. A young woman, obviously pregnant, met them at the door and then seated them at a table where they could see the truck when John asked.

"Mother Corrin said you'd paid for a meal. I'll have it right out." She came back a couple minutes later with two glasses, a pitcher of water, cloth napkins, and flatware. "The water is filtered."

Another quick trip and she was setting two large bowls of mulligan stew, and surprisingly, a small loaf of fresh bread, on the table. "Sorry. No butter to spare."

"This is fine," a wan looking John said, smiling up at the woman's face. "Thank you."

The young woman smiled back and nodded, and then left them to their meal.

They ate slowly, savoring the thick, aromatic stew. It didn't have an overabundance of meat, but there was some, and plenty of carrots, potatoes, and onions. When they were done, John said, "Leave a tip." He shrugged. "Couple of dimes."

Belinda nodded and did so. The young woman saw them rising from the table and came over. "Everything all right?"

Belinda smile and said, "It was great. Thank you."

When they were back in the room, it was already dark. Belinda set up the MSR stove and heated water to make hot lemonade for John. She added a small dollop of Everclear to the cup of lemonade and handed it to John.

"You better take the bathroom first," John said, taking a tiny sip of the toddy. "Between this and a hot bath, I'm going to be out of it."

Belinda wanted to argue, but John was probably right. He could still function at the moment, but later that might be different. "Take your time," John said as she entered the bathroom with her pack.

Taking John at his word, Belinda took a long bath, a luxury she hadn't been able to experience in a very long time. She dried off and dressed again. When John entered the bathroom, Belinda went out and set up the perimeter alarms and the truck alarm. When she reentered the room, she went to the bathroom door and called out to John, "You okay in there," afraid he might fall asleep in the tub.

"Yeah. Just a little longer."

"Take your time. Just don't fall asleep in there," Belinda replied. She went to the beds and turned them both back, and then waited for John to reappear. She was about ready to call to him again, but the bathroom door opened and he walked out wearing his boxer shorts, rubbing his head vigorously with a towel. His hair was almost as long as Belinda's. It was the first time she'd seen it down. He usually had it in a ponytail.

John fell into bed, covered up, and was asleep in moments. Belinda read until ten, when the lights went out. It took her a while to fall asleep.

When Belinda woke the next morning, John wasn't in his bed. She used the bathroom and went looking for him. She found him in the restaurant, talking to several men. They all had cups of tea, by the lack of the smell. It wasn't coffee.

John motioned her over, but didn't introduce her. "Tea?" he asked and she nodded. John signaled the server, the same woman as the night before. She hurried over with another cup and saucer.

There was a plastic honey bear dispenser bottle on the table. It was nearly empty and Belinda took only one squeeze to add honey to the tea. She couldn't identify it, but it tasted good.

The men all finished their tea and got up, leaving the table to John and Belinda. Betty, the server, came over and asked if they were ready for breakfast.

John nodded and Betty hurried away. She seemed to only have two speeds. Stopped and in a hurry. She was back a couple minutes later, with a serving tray. She set out bowls of steaming rice, a pitcher of milk, and another honey bear.

The two ate slowly, in silence, enjoying their tea and rice. When they were done, Betty cleared the table. "Time to be off," John said. "You have the pouch?"

Belinda nodded and handed it to John. "I offered to buy the tea for the morning coffee klatch this morning." He counted out two silver halves, two silver quarters, and two silver dimes and left on the table as he rose. "Betty said the breakfast was included, but I added a bit, anyway," John told Belinda as they headed for the front door.

Belinda saw Betty and the older woman standing in the door leading to the kitchen and called back, "Thanks for everything!" The two waved in response.

As they approached the truck, Belinda said, "You seem to be much better this morning."

"Yeah. Feels really good to feel better, if you know what I mean."

Belinda laughed. "I think I do. You want me to drive?"

"I'll drive. Things should be smooth sailing for a while, according to the news I got before breakfast. Up past Ft. Leonard Wood. Rolla. I'll want you behind the wheel when we get close to Rolla. There are rumors of trouble there."

"Can we go around?"

"We may just do that. Depends on what the military at the Fort have to say."

They stopped short of the Fort, pulling into one of the entrances to a section of Mark Twain National Forest. They were surprised to find the kiosk manned, though the person wasn't wearing a Park uniform. He was armed, but was friendly.

"No room for permanent residents. We do have a couple of openings for transients. You have to pay your way. Food, medicine, or fuel."

"How much fuel for an overnight?" John asked.

"Gallon of gas or gallon and a half of diesel," was the reply.

"Diesel," John replied, getting out of the truck. The man had a gallon can marked for diesel handy and John filled the can. The man emptied it into a jerry can and then John half-filled the can again from one of the barrels in the trailer.

He gave John directions to the lots set aside for travelers and said, "Mind your manners and there won't be any trouble. Any trades you do are at your own risk. We have a lot of good people here, but there are a handful of less than trustworthy. But they have kids and we won't throw them out.

The area was filled with people. From the looks of some of the camps, people had been there since the war. There was still forest, but upon closer inspection, many trees outside of the actual campground had been cut down, presumably for firewood. Some of those open areas were also occupied with a vast variety of tents and vehicles, including several semi-trailers.

John and Belinda had barely started setting up their camp when several people stopped by. It was about an equal mix of men and women, with the occasional teen. "You trading?" asked one of those in the front of the group.

"Might," John replied. "What are you offering?"

Everyone started clamoring for attention and John held up his hands. "One at a time. Please." Again it was pandemonium. "Hold it! Hold it!" John said. "Look. We'll lay down a tarp with what we have to trade here in a little while. You can come by as the evening progresses and see if you want to trade anything for what we have."

With some muttering the growing crowd broke up and people moved away. "Are you sure you want to do this?" Belinda asked as the finished setting up camp. They'd already stopped for their evening meal, so as soon as the tents were set up, John laid down a tarp and put a few things out on it. Belinda brought out some of her trade goods and added them to the tarp.

A few people had been lurking close and immediately came forward when John unfolded a director's chair and sat down by the tarp. He had his Benelli M4 shotgun handy, as well as wearing the P-14. Belinda also had her weapons in evidence, following John's lead.

There was immediate interest in John's display of 200ml bottles of 190 proof Everclear, the 1.5 ounce packets of Prince Albert tobacco, the OCB rolling papers, and the small boxes of wooden matches. There was also an open box of Folgers Coffee Singles.

Belinda on the other hand had a rapidly growing group of women and girls interested in her feminine hygiene supplies, personal care items, collection of bras and panties, needles and thread, and makeup.

Of interest, though less so, were some of the basics that John set out. One pound boxes or bags of beans, rice, sugar, and salt. Cans of meat. While he had quite a bit to trade, he only put out one or two of each item. He didn't want anyone to know how much he did have.

LOW PROFILE

It didn't take long for the crowd to swell as word went around the encampment. The trading went slowly. People didn't have that much to trade away and everyone wanted the maximum they could get for the least they had to give.

Belinda looked up quickly when a woman offered her 'services' to John for one of the bottles of Everclear. Belinda noted there was a man with her. He looked as eager for the alcohol as she did. John declined and the two moved off, dejectedly.

Like John, Belinda kept scanning the area for trouble. She caught John's eye a few minutes later and nodded toward the man and woman returning. The man had one hand in the pocket of his light jacket.

When Belinda looked over at John again she noted the empty holster for his P-14. She couldn't see his hands, either.

When the man pulled a handgun from the jacket pocket everyone froze. Belinda glanced over at John again. She could tell from his posture now he was holding the P-14 at the ready. But the man asked, "How much for this?" and held out the revolver toward John. "A bottle?"

"Any ammo?" John asked, taking the revolver. Everyone seemed to relax.

"Just what's in it," replied the man.

"Please?" the woman as much as begged.

"Okay," John said. "One bottle." He picked up the bottle of Everclear and handed it to the man. John called after them as the pair scurried away, "Be sure and cut it with something. It's 190 proof."

The trading went on until dark. Quite a few people had gardens going in various parts of the Park and John and Belinda both got several items of fresh food in trade. They each picked up a weapon each, with some ammunition. John got some spare parts off vehicles that wouldn't run that would work on his truck.

John noticed one man off to the side that had been eyeing the tarp almost from the start. He was on crutches and looked like death warmed over.

As the man started to turn away and leave, John asked, "You looking to trade for something?"

"Some of the food. But I ain't got nothing to trade, but some gold and silver and won't nobody take it around here."

"Coins?" John asked.

The man nodded.

"We'll take it," John replied. "All you have, if you prefer to invest in some trade goods besides the food."

The man's eyes lit up, and he came closer. "Truly?"

John nodded.

"Ain't got much, but I'll trade off all I got for food and trade goods. A couple that said they would take gold wouldn't make change and all I have is one-ounce Krugerrands and Gold Eagles and one-ounce Silver Eagles. They want a full coin for just a couple meals worth of food. No one else here will take it. Always hear 'you can't eat gold'."

"Was a lot of people's opinion before the war," John replied. "Wouldn't get any. Then I know one guy that decided that was the only thing he would need. Don't know how he's fared."

"That's what I did. Then got stuck here on a cross country RV trip. Me and my daughter. She died." After a pause the man spoke again. "You seem to be making good trades. You won't cheat me, will you?"

"Of course not," Belinda replied.

"I'll go get it. Could you wait a few more minutes before you put up your stuff?"

"We'll wait," John replied.

A few minutes later the man returned, carrying a small fire safe. "Got it in here," he told John and handed the safe to him.

John opened the safe up with the key the man handed him, and whistled when he saw the gleam of gold even in the fading light. "When did you get this?"

"'99. Before Y2K. Nothing happened and I just put it away. Should have sold it and bought food," the man added with a shake of his head.

"Paid around three hundred an ounce for the gold, I take it," John said.

The man nodded.

"You have a place to keep things safe?" John asked.

Again, the man nodded. "Got a big motorhome back a-ways, out of the way. Won't run. Generator ran until I traded away all the diesel for food."

"Okay. Here's what I'm willing to do. I have quite a bit more to trade than I'm showing. I'll pull around where you are and we can move stuff from the truck and trailer to your motorhome."

"How much stuff?" the man asked, very curious.

"Enough to keep you in trade goods for a long time, if you're careful."

Belinda helped John loaded the things from the tarp into the back of the truck.

John asked the man. "What's your name?"

"Alexander Levine. Everyone calls me Xander."

John shook his hand and said, "I'm John. This is Belinda. Climb in the cab and I'll be right there."

When Xander was in the truck, John took Belinda aside and asked her, "How much of your trade goods you want to part with? Any amount up to all of it."

"He's got that much gold?"

John nodded.

"Three-quarters?" Belinda asked. "Across the board."

"That's good. I'll make up the rest. Keep an eye out. I'll be back in a little while." John went to the truck and climbed in the driver's side and started the truck. Xander gave him directions and they were soon at Xander's motorhome.

John began to carry box after box of trade goods into the motorhome, as Xander watched incredulously after the first three.

"What I gave you is all I have," Xander said when John picked up yet another box.

"I know. Gold is worth more now than the three-hundred you paid for it."

When John had moved three-quarters of Belinda's stuff, he moved half of his. "This going to be all right with you?" he asked, finally stopping and standing by Xander at the door of the motorhome.

"My yes! I didn't expect a tenth of what you have given me."

"Like I said, gold is worth more now than you paid for it. A lot more. We're coming out of this smelling like a rose."

"Well, if you're happy," Xander said, "I sure am." He held out his hand again and John shook it.

"One more thing," John said, getting into the back of the truck again. He came back out and handed Xander the revolver he'd traded for. "I happened to have a couple of boxes of ammunition for this. I don't use this caliber. Just in case you need it. I wouldn't let on I had as much as you do."

"Like you did, huh? Thank you," Xander replied, tears in his eyes. "I think you may have just saved my life."

With a wave Xander probably couldn't see in the dark, John climbed back in the truck and went back to the camp. As soon as he was parked, he helped Belinda set out the perimeter alarm system.

"I hate to say this, but with this many people here, and them knowing we have trade goods, I think we'd better keep a watch, besides just the alarms."

"I'm not surprised. Normally you would do like we do for supper. Eat one place and camp another. You'd do the trading, but not hang around."

"That's right. But we're here and I don't want to look for a better place in the dark."

"Can I have first watch?" Belinda asked.

John smiled at her and nodded. He showed her the open fire safe. "Fifty each one-ounce gold coins and one-ounce silver rounds. He counted out the coins in the light of the moon through the high haze. "You get 15 each one-ounce gold coins and one-ounce silver rounds. Don't like the rounds. Prefer the US silver coins. But someone will take them somewhere."

John stashed his gold and silver before he went to bed, using the several hiding places he had in, on, and under the truck.

There was no trouble during Belinda's watch that night, but John spotted someone moving about outside the range of the perimeter alarms. John was using the night vision goggles. He took a small laser pointer from his breast pocket and shined it toward the person in the woods. The red dot appeared brightly on the person's chest. Whoever it was moved away, making much more noise than he or she had done getting close.

CHAPTER ELEVEN

The next morning John woke Belinda up early and they broke camp and loaded up before first light. John left the makings for a hot breakfast out and they prepared it on the tailgate of the truck. As they finished it and Belinda was putting the rest of the hot tea in John's thermos people began showing up, asking for additional trades.

"Sorry," John said. "All traded out." The crowd did not look nearly as friendly as they had the night before.

"Xander had a little gold. He bought what we had left on the tarp," John told the group. "You might see if he'll do some trading." John pulled on to the Park road and headed for the entrance.

"You think Xander will be okay? Those people don't look happy," Belinda said.

"I think he'll be fine. I kind of suggested he keep it low profile."

It didn't take long to get to the section of I-44 that Ft. Leonard Wood was controlling. The sentries at the blockade were polite and efficient when John handed one of them their traveling papers.

"It is not required, but if you can spare some fuel, it would be appreciated," the second sentry said as the first one went over the papers.

"Five gallons of diesel?" John asked.

The sentry looked amazed. "Absolutely! I'll get a jerry can."

John pumped the fuel from a drum into the sentry's can. "What can you tell me about Rolla? I've heard there are problems."

"Yes. We don't know the extent of it. We're trying to find out more. If you have fuel and you can, I suggest you by-pass Rolla, even with these documents. We can no longer vouch for the military forces stationed there." He looked grim.

"I understand," John said, accepting the papers when they were handed back to him. The two sentries pushed the car in the opening of the blockade out of the way and waved John through.

After driving out of sight of the checkpoint, John stopped and took out one of his maps. After studying it for a while he pointed out the route he intended to take. "State 28 north through Dixon and then state 68 south through Vichy to I-44 again. It's a long ways out of the way, but we have the time and the fuel to do it. I think better safe than sorry."

"That's fine with me," Belinda said. "You want me to drive part of it?"

"Sure. Doubt if there will be a problem. You might as well drive part of the time just on general principles. I kind of got used to just riding along." John grinned over at Belinda. They switched seats and Belinda drove toward the other blockade the military from Ft. Leonard Wood controlled.

Apparently, the sentries at the first blockade had radioed ahead for the blockade was already open. The sentries waved them through. Belinda had to change over to the west bound lanes once, as the east bound were blocked from the median to the side ditch. It made her uncomfortable and she switched back to the eastbound lanes as soon as she could.

The interchange with Highway 28 wasn't far and Belinda took the exit. It was blocked. "You want to get us around this?" she asked John.

He smiled at her and said, "No. You're doing okay."

Belinda wended their way around, finally getting back on the interstate and crossing the median and then the other ditch. She stopped and John got out. He cut the fence with the cutters from the tool box and climbed back in the truck.

There were signs of activity in Dixon, but they didn't stop and no one tried to interfere with them. The continued northeast until they hit Highway 68. That took them back southeast. It was going to be right at dark if they continued to Vichy so they stopped even earlier than usual.

They went through Vichy early the next morning. Like Dixon, there were no blockades or sentries. Just a few people here and there. They didn't stop. They ran into the same situation when they got close to Sullivan. John didn't want to arrive at dusk. They got off the Interstate and set up camp. There should be a military presence in Sullivan. A small one. And Colonel Andrew's family lived just outside of the city. They wanted to have a full day to get done what they needed.

It took a little more than a day. It took almost the full day to get clearance to enter the city. The Lieutenant in charge of the two platoons in Sullivan was green. He tried to contact his superior, but the Captain he reported to was out in the field somewhere. Finally, after a five-hour wait, the Lieutenant finally signed off on the papers and let John and Belinda enter his jurisdiction.

They went ahead and left the Interstate to go into Sullivan proper. There was quite a bit of activity. John was at the wheel and he drove around town until he found a city park that looked promising as an overnight spot.

LOW PROFILE

It wasn't long after they set up camp that people began to stop in, ostensibly to say hello. John told Belinda, "I think they want to check us out for either being a problem or a resource."

"You think we should try to do some trading?"

"We'd better ask," John replied, waving at a couple riding horses coming toward them. "That Lieutenant doesn't have his act together. I don't want to break some silly rule and get held more than we already have."

When the couple approaching were within talking distance John said, "Hello! How are you?"

The two exchanged a glance and the man said, "Well as can be expected. You?"

"Good. We're here delivering some mail."

"Like in the movie 'Postman'?" The woman asked, looking interested.

"No," replied John. "Just some personal papers a friend asked us to drop off."

Both looked disappointed. "It would be nice if there was postal service, at least. No phone... No mail... It's difficult."

"Do you have an Amateur Radio for communications?

The man shook his head. "Always planned to get one. Never did. I'm Jim Thompson, by the way. And this is my wife Helen."

They all shook hands. "I'm John and this is Belinda. I have a question? Is it okay to barter here in Sullivan or is that restricted?"

"Well," Jim said, "It is preferred that it be done over at the high school. Supposed to pay a fee to trade. Like the old swap meet booth rental."

John looked over at Belinda. "I think I'd rather pass," she said.

Looking back at Jim, John then asked, "They using precious metals much, or just straight barter?"

"Some of both," replied Jim. "We trade honey. Prefer food and gas. Are you traders?"

"We do a little," John said. But probably not here. We're only stopping off to drop off those papers."

"If you change your mind, the high school isn't far. We'll be there tomorrow morning."

That was the general sentiment as several more people stopped by to check the newcomers.

"Watches again?" Belinda asked, when they were getting ready to settle in for the night.

"I don't think it is really necessary… but, yeah. You want first watch again?"

"If you don't mind."

"No. Fine with me. I'll see you at two."

John had been right. No one approached after they turned off the lights they were using. Belinda woke up to brewing coffee and the sight of a man in a city police uniform talking to John.

"Belinda," John said, motioning her over. "This is Officer Paul Hickman. Local constabulary. He's been filling me in on the situation here in Sullivan."

"Officer Hickman," Belinda said, shaking his hand. She looked over at John. "Anything I should know about?"

John shook his head. "They do take their trading seriously. Quite a few people, according to Officer Hickman, aren't pleased with the tax and may try to trade with us outside the regular trading area."

Belinda looked a little concerned. Knowing John's nature fairly well, there was a distinct possibility he might want to do something about that tax.

Seeming to read her mind, John smiled and said, "Don't worry. I'm not about to start a tax revolt. But it is information that Colonel Andrews will want to know.

Officer Hickman has agreed to keep an eye on things and report them to the Colonel by radio. He's an Amateur himself."

"Just a couple of basic radios," Paul protested. "I'm not even sure my system will reach Tulsa. I've heard them a few times, but never tried to go back to them."

"Well do it if you can," replied John. "For our part, we need to finish up here and go find the Colonel's family. You take care, Officer." John shook Paul's hand again and Paul turned back to his horse.

"Lot of horses," Belinda commented. "What does his make? Twelve? Fourteen?"

"Something like that," John said. "Good way of getting around locally. With the honey, and number of horses, it makes me think the area didn't get much fallout from Whiteman. I figured the base and missile silos would get hit hard, even though the silos are supposed to be empty."

"There are missile silos in Missouri? I didn't know that." Belinda looked a little pale.

"They were deactivated in the mid-'90's. But I always thought they might get hit, anyway, in an all-out war. Apparently, I was wrong. Which is good. Let's finish up and get going."

A little while later, with John driving, they headed toward Colonel Andrews' family's home. The Colonel had sketched out a map. It was easy to follow. They pulled into a long driveway well before noon. There was no gate or visible sentries, but John drove slowly and carefully up the driveway.

There seemed to be garden plots everywhere. John stopped, opened the door of the truck and stepped out with one foot. He beeped the horn and called out, "Hello the house!"

He saw the curtains move in a window and waited, somewhat anxiously, for someone to respond. Finally the front door of the house opened slightly and a woman's voice sounded. "Who are you and what do you want?"

"We're looking for Dania Perkins. We have a message from Colonel Thaddeus Andrews."

The door opened wider and an elderly woman stepped out. She had long gray hair. John could just make out someone behind her. He caught the gleam of gun metal and was careful to stay motionless.

"Why should we believe you?"

"The Colonel said I should bring up June, 2001. You'd know he sent me."

The woman hurried down the steps of the porch that surrounded the farm house.

"Is he all right? Why did he send you?"

When John stepped the rest of the way out of the truck, the woman holding a shotgun behind the gray-haired woman stepped out onto the porch, holding the shotgun down to her side.

"I'm Dania," said the gray-haired woman. "That's Thad's wife with the shotgun. Courtney. She's my daughter. What is it you have for me?"

Belinda handed the large manila envelope to John and he handed it to Dania. She started to open it, but suddenly looked up at John. "Oh. Pardon my manners. Please. Come into the house and have a cup of tea. Lunch will be ready shortly."

"Mother," Courtney said in a rather chiding voice.

"Oh, honey! I'm sure it is okay. We can afford a little food for someone bringing messages from your husband."

Courtney stepped out of the way when Dania led John and Belinda into the house. "See to the lunch, dear," Dania told her daughter as they all entered the large country kitchen the house boasted.

Finally, after another glance at John and Belinda, Courtney set aside the shotgun and busied herself in kitchen as Dania, John, and Belinda sat down around the kitchen table.

Dania fumbled a bit, but finally got the envelope open. When the coins slid out, making a racket on the wooden table, Courtney looked around. She saw the coins and began to smile, seemingly quite relieved about something.

"Oh, my!" Dania said and then quickly withdrew three regular #10 envelopes.

John could see Dania's name on one, Courtney's on another and the third with two boys' names. Dania handed Courtney's envelope to her and tore open her own envelope. Both women began to read, suddenly oblivious to John and Belinda.

Both women shed a few tears while they read. John and Belinda sat quietly. Finally Dania wiped her eyes and looked up. "You don't know what it means to hear from Thaddeus."

Courtney said essentially the same, looking much happier than she had. "I'm going to take the boys' letter out to them," she said, scurrying out the back door of the house.

"This is the best news we've had in a long time," Dania said, finally looking up from her letter. "I don't know how to repay you for bringing this."

"Not to worry," John said with a smile. "Colonel Andrews paid the postage."

"Oh. Well, I still insist you stay for lunch."

"We will," John said, looking at Belinda first and getting a nod. "If you insist. And if there is something you want to send back to the Colonel, I do plan on going back that way, eventually."

"No," Dania replied. "Thad sent instructions on how we can contact him through the military in town."

Courtney came back inside the kitchen and quickly put together sandwiches for John and Belinda. "We don't get much meat," she said, setting the plate of sandwiches on the table. "It's alfalfa sprouts and tomato on fresh bread."

"Sounds excellent," John said, transferring one of the sandwiches to his plate, as Belinda did the same. "Looks like you have quite the garden going," he said after his first bite. "And this is excellent."

"Yes," Dania replied. "The gardens are what have kept us going. Courtney and I do quite well, but it's really the boys that have the green thumbs. I think they were born to be farmers."

"Very good profession in today's world," Belinda said.

Courtney was still making sandwiches. A few minutes later two young men, looking to be in their mid-teens, entered to the standard mother's admonishment, "Get washed up for lunch."

Both left the kitchen, to return one at a time to take seats around at the table.

"Thanks for bringing the letters," the eldest, Thaddeus, told John.

"Yes," added the other, Joshua. "What's it like out there?" he asked, making a vague gesture indicating the outside world.

"It can be tough," John replied truthfully. "But people like your father are making things better. And people like you, producing food, are all helping bring things back to a modicum of normal."

"More?" Courtney asked when John finished the first sandwich. Belinda was just finishing her sandwich, too. "How about you?" Belinda shook her head.

"We need to get back on our journey," John said, rising from the table. Belinda stood as well.

"I'll show you out," Dania said, also rising. She stopped at the front door. "Thank you for what you have done. You'll always be welcome here."

"Thank you," John and Belinda both said. Without a look back, John walked out to the truck, Belinda following.

"They seem to be doing okay," Belinda said as John turned the truck and trailer around and headed down the driveway.

"Yeah. Must be tough. I hope the gold the Colonel sent them helps out. Those boys could use a little meat, to put some meat on their bones."

"I noticed that, too. All of them are thin."

They got back on I-44 and headed east again. This time there was no problem passing though the blockade east of Sullivan. Apparently, the word had made it to the Lieutenant that the papers were to be honored, and honored quickly. He had left orders for the men on duty to expedite John and Belinda through the blockade.

They traveled until near dark before John stopped for them to prepare their supper. Afterwards they traveled another few miles and stopped at a place John knew where he thought they could camp. The small quarter-acre 'ranchette' was deserted and the house ransacked and partially burned.

"I hope they are doing okay somewhere," John said, looking grim. "They were good people. Had decent preps. You just never know. Let's get out of here." John drove them a bit further and they set up camp just off the road at the junction with the Interstate.

Belinda looked distracted the next morning as they had breakfast and then broke camp. "You okay?" John asked her.

"I don't know," she replied softly. "I don't know what to expect. The Colonel's family is doing fine, but your friends are nowhere to be found. My parents..." her voice trailed away, tears glistening in her eyes.

Softly, John said, "There is still hope. You said your parents are resourceful. You have done fine through all of this. There is a good chance they will have as well. We'll find out today."

Belinda nodded and they got into the truck. John drove and when they got close, Belinda began to give him directions to get to her parents' place just outside of Robertsville. John glanced over at her when she said, "Next driveway..." She looked like she would shatter if he touched her, she was so tense.

Rather like the Colonel's family's place and their gardens everywhere, there seemed to be clotheslines everywhere on Belinda's family's small property. And stacks of cut and split wood.

"Someone is here," John said. "And taking in washing, from the looks of it."

John had barely come to a stop when Belinda hopped out of the truck and ran toward a woman that had just come out from behind a line of wash. "Mother!" Belinda nearly screamed, running to gather the woman up in a huge hug.

John saw a man rumble from the house. He looked strong as an ox, despite his apparent age. The man gathered both the woman and Belinda in a bear hug. John got out of the truck and approached the group. He saw tears in all their eyes and had to blink back some of his own.

He stayed out of the way as they all began to cry openly when Belinda told them about what had happened during and after the war. Belinda's father helped her mother into the house and Belinda turned to John.

"I'm sorry... Haven't even introduced you yet."

"Don't worry about it. Take all the time you need. I understand."

"At least come inside and sit down," Belinda replied, leading John toward the sprawling ranch style house.

It was a few more minutes before Belinda began to introduce John to her parents, Betty and Richard Sharp. Suddenly John's hand was on the butt of the P-14. He'd seen a man at one of the doors, peeking through. He had a gun.

"No! Wait!" Richard said. "That's Allen. Allen, come on in here. Everything is all right. Look who is here."

A slender man, about John's age, with a decided limp, walked into the living room, holstering his pistol. John took his hand off the P-14.

"Allen?" Belinda asked, looking bewildered. "What are you doing here?"

"He's been helping out," Richard said.

"He's been a godsend," said Betty, looking over at Allen fondly.

"Allen, this is John. John, Allen." The two men shook hands.

"If you're responsible for getting Belinda back to her family, I thank you," Allen said, looking John over as carefully as John was looking him over.

"And we add our heartfelt thanks to that," Richard said as the two men stepped back from one another.

"Allen," Belinda suddenly said, "Your wife..."

"She was in St. Louis," Allen said.

"Oh, I'm so sorry," Belinda replied, going over to take his hand.

"I'll let the four of you catch up," John said, turning toward the door.

Belinda started to stop him, but her mother, father, and Allen all started talking to her at once and John was gone before she could ask him to stay.

It was nearly an hour later when Belinda came out of the house to invite John in for lunch. She saw her belongings stacked neatly by the front door of the house. John was in the trailer, transferring fuel from one of the drums to the truck.

John nodded and finished up the fuelling before he put the pump away and hopped down out of the trailer. "Show me where to wash up."

"Allen found some solar panels," Belinda said. "The water pump works so the bathrooms work okay. We even have hot… rather, warm, water. Allen made some water heating panels."

John came out of the bathroom a few minutes later and joined the four in the kitchen. They weren't crying anymore. There was even some laughter as they reminisced about old times. John learned that Allen and Belinda had almost married at one time. From the looks of it, John thought, Allen was still carrying a torch, despite the fact that each had married someone else. And Belinda seemed to be responding to it.

He also learned how Allen had helped out the Sharps during and after the war. To get them some power and water. To help get Betty going with a clothes washing service and Richard a firewood service. The help he was to get goats, rabbits, and chickens started to supply them with meat and additional income. And all the fishing in the nearby river. The hunting and trapping. All which he shared with the Sharps.

"What about the farm, Dad? The fields look planted."

Richard sighed. "I had to let Harry Brown take it over. Even with Allen, I couldn't manage any more. We butchered all the stock and traded it off since we couldn't keep it. Harry is giving us a quarter of what he makes for the use of the land."

After the light lunch, John went out to set up his camp. The Sharps had invited him to stay for as long as he wanted. Belinda came out a few minutes later to talk to him. "John, I know I had left it open about whether or not I would be staying, even if we found my parents. I've already decided to stay, now that I am here. They need my help."

John nodded. "I think you are making the right decision."

There was a long silence as Belinda studied John's implacable face. "Are you going to stay in the area?" she finally asked.

John shook his head. "No. I'll be going back, eventually. I've some things to check on while I'm in the area, but I don't plan to stay."

They both felt the wall go up between them. The easy companionship was gone. They were just two acquaintances now, not the fast friends they had become. John left the next morning, leaving behind one of the Amateur radios and a broadband antenna they'd scavenged so Belinda could stay in touch. With the Farm.

CHAPTER TWELVE

It wasn't that far to St. Louis, he had travel permits for the city, and John still had plenty of biodiesel. He was feeling a little restless and a little reckless. John decided to head to the city and see if he could scavenge anything of value.

There was a much larger military presence around St. Louis than Tulsa. He had no trouble getting past the cordon, but was cautioned about looting. John kept an eye on the radiation survey meter on the console beside him. Also beside him was an open St. Louis yellow pages telephone directory. He headed for the nearest coin shop.

He passed the first roving patrol without problems. When he passed the second, the reading on the survey meter started climbing quickly. John came to his senses and turned around, headed out of St. Louis. Scavenging was one thing. When the powers that be declared it looting and used force to back it up, he was a fool if he tried it.

It was late afternoon when he passed the east side blockade on I-44 and left military jurisdiction. He almost decided to just head back to the Farm as quickly as possible, but as he relaxed from tension he didn't realize he was feeling, John slowed the truck down and planned to get to his property outside Stanton the following morning.

There were more caves in Missouri than just the famous Onondaga Cave and the more infamous Meramec

Caverns that Jessie James had once used as a hide out. John owned a piece of land with a relatively small non-commercial cave. The five acres were heavily wooded and bordered on a small year round spring fed creek.

John had to maneuver the truck carefully with the trailer to get to the cave's location. There was a gully down slope from the cave's main entrance. John had done quite a bit of shovel work on it in the past and could park the truck in it, even with the trailer. When the truck and trailer were covered with the camouflage tarps, they were nearly invisible.

HK-91 slung over his shoulder, John hiked up to the cave entrance he normally used. It was basically a small hole in the ground at the base of a steeper rise than that below it. There were two other entrances that John had found when he'd explored the cave after he'd found it when he was looking for land in the area.

Both were similar holes in the ground, one a mile away to the north and the other just under a mile to the east. Both the other properties were vacant when John had bought his property. He promptly installed solid steel barriers inside all three entrances for liability reasons as well as security.

John slid down the short distance from the ground level to the point where the barrier was. He manipulated the hidden catch on one side of the steel grate and swung it open. He had to crouch down to fit in the passage. John turned on his five D-cell Maglite. The passage sloped slightly and though dry, the bare rock could be a bit slick. But the lugs on his Matterhorn boots gripped tightly and he had no trouble reaching the one large room he'd found in the cave.

The room was only a little over seven feet high in most places, and measured approximately twenty by thirty feet in size. There were a half a dozen openings in walls and floor. The one in the floor was just large enough to get into, but tapered like a funnel to just six inches in diameter.

Three of the passages opening into the wall were essentially dead ends, though they all had small openings leading out of them much too small for a person to travel. The other two passages were winding courses gradually leading downward to the openings on the other two properties. Each had a series of small rooms in that length that ranged in size from six by eight to ten by twelve. Only in the big room was there standup headroom for more than a few feet in any direction. All the passages, except the short one from his entrance to the large room, were rather narrow, in addition to having low overhead room.

The cave was dry, with no signs of water intrusion in even the heaviest rains that the area was occasionally prone. No stalagmites, nor stalactites. Most importantly, no signs of bats, though there had been some signs of small animals initially. Nothing since he'd put in the barriers.

John found the windup LED flashlight and cranked it a few times. When he had light from it he turned off the Maglite. Though he had distributed some of the supplies and equipment in the other small rooms of the cave, the majority were in the large room. Most were in commercial shipping cases, despite the dryness of the cave.

There was also a row of 15-gallon drums of water lined up against one wall. Two more of the water drums were in the smaller rooms close by, along with a chemical toilet and a rolling waste tote. John's plan was to transfer the waste from the toilet to the tote, and then take the tote outside to bury the waste.

It took a while to check the entire cavern. Everything was just as he'd left it. He'd really only intended to check the place and then leave, but John found himself settling down for the evening. He went back to the truck and brought back his main pack and the computer case after resetting the alarms on the truck and perimeter alarms around the entrance.

He set up one of the half-a-dozen cots and got out wool blankets from one of the shipping crates. John had an aluminum roll-up table as part of the equipment and set it up, too, along with a folding chair. It was absolutely silent in the cave, except for the sound of his breathing, and then the slight whirr of John's laptop computer.

John spent the rest of the day reading, until time for supper. After he prepared and ate his supper, feeling as safe and relaxed as he had in a long time, John pulled out the stainless-steel flask he kept in his pack. Though he had one for medicinal 190 proof Everclear, this flask was filled with Hennessy Paradis Extra cognac.

He took a few sips as he continued to read after his supper. John carefully recapped the flask and put it away before he went to bed.

It was storming the next morning, though John didn't know it until he headed to the truck with the things he'd brought in the evening before. Seeing that nothing had been disturbed during the night, John decided to spend the day at the cave. He turned around and went back to the main room and made himself comfortable.

When he checked again late that afternoon, it had stopped raining. John went down to the truck and turned on the Yaesu FT-897D to see if he could raise the Farm. The Yaesu ATAS 120 broadband antenna did its job and John was soon talking to Adam. He winced a bit when Adam read him the riot act for not checking in more often.

John apologized and then filled Adam in on what had transpired the last few days. "Are you doing okay?" Adam asked, rather solicitously.

"Sure. Why wouldn't I be?" John replied, a bit surprised at Adam's question.

"No reason. Just asking." After a pause Adam asked, "When you think you'll be home?"

"A few days," John replied. "It took us a bit longer than I anticipated getting to Belinda's parents, what with the weather and me getting sick. I'll be back in plenty of time to help with the harvest."

Adam held his tongue and didn't blast John. He decided that if John said he was all right, then he was all right. Adam signed off and John did the same. John reset the alarms and went back to the cave for the evening.

It was 3:05 AM by John's watch when something woke him up. He started to get up from the cot, but was thrown off as the cot turned over. John grabbed the 91 when he realized the remote monitors for the perimeter alarms and the truck alarms were sounding off.

There was another sound and John slowly realized it was the rock itself making the noise. "Earthquake!" John said aloud. He scrambled for the entrance of the cave. It was a warm, still night, except the trees were shaking and the ground was, too.

John managed to stand as he felt wave after wave of movement pass beneath his bare feet. The movements died away and John hurried back into the cave to get dressed. He knew he shouldn't be so worried about being in the cave. It had withstood the 1811-1812 earthquakes. No reason to believe it wouldn't survive this one, bad as it appeared to be.

Leaving the cave gear where it was, John took his pack and computer back to the trailer and gathered up the perimeter alarms to put them away. John started the truck and began calling for the Farm on their nighttime frequency. Sally Ridenour answered almost immediately.

"John, are you feeling that?" she asked as soon as she recognized John's call.

"I hope to tell you! You're feeling it, too?"

"Things are shaking all over here!"

"Just ride it out," John said. "That's all we can do. As soon as you see him let Adam know I'm okay." John jumped when a tree nearby with a damaged root structure came tumbling down, narrowly missing the hood of the truck. John wasn't going anywhere until he cleared away that tree.

There were aftershocks off and on for over an hour. After an hour of silence and stillness, John contacted Sally again. "Seems to be over here for the moment," John said.

"Here, too. Been over an hour since the last big shock."

John signed off again and just sat in the truck, waiting for daylight. When it was light enough, he got out of the truck and got the chainsaw out of a toolbox. It took another hour to cut up the tree and get it out of the way so he could move the truck. He was very careful to maintain a stance so if there was another earthquake, he wouldn't injure himself with the chainsaw.

He took the time to stack the wood for future use, but then drove the truck and trailer up out of the gully. Though toppling trees were still a possibility if there were more shakes, John felt better about having the truck where he could move it more easily.

Having hurriedly abandoned the cave, John went back inside and checked everything one last time before he locked up the entrance. He was ready to leave when another shock shook the area, for almost as long as the first, and nearly as powerful. John saw three more trees go down, but none close to him.

John worked his way back to the nearest road, once having to use the chainsaw again to clear a path, and once using the front winch to pull a tree out of the way. He made it back to the Interstate before another quake shook the truck. He stopped as quickly as he could and rode the shaking out.

The first overpass on the I-44 he came to was down. He used the entrance and exit ramps to bypass it. It became the norm. Almost all the overpasses were down. John made it to Sullivan and checked in with the military authorities, telling them what he'd seen and experienced. They confirmed that it was a widespread earthquake due to the New Madrid Fault System.

Everywhere he went structural damage was great. Houses and barns down or partially down. Some burned.

John was glad he'd brought as much diesel with him as he had, and then refueled in Lebanon. From the looks of things, it was going to be a long slow ride back to Tulsa. He was right. Downed bridges caused a lot more problems than downed overpasses. He was traveling side roads more than he was Interstate. It worked out fine, going around Rolla. He would have done that anyway.

He was running on fumes when he pulled into Big Mike's Chevron station in Lebanon three weeks later, looking for biodiesel. Big Mike came out to meet John, when John pulled in and parked beside the fuel tank truck.

"There was a lady with you before," Mike said as John got out of the truck.

"Yeah. I was taking her to her parents' place to check on them. She decided to stay."

"Too bad," Mike replied. "She was good looking."

"Yeah. Very capable, too. What do you have in the way of biodiesel?"

"I've quite a bit, but with things the way they are, I'm trying to keep it for locals."

"I see," John said slowly.

"That's not to mean I won't sell you some, but there will be a premium."

John nodded. He'd planned on filling everything, just in case, but if Big Mike was going to gouge him, John would only take enough to get him back to the Farm. As it turned out, John was able to fill the cross bed 100-gallon tank and three of the five 55-gallon drums for five ounces of gold coins.

He skipped the motel and restaurant this time, leaving Lebanon early enough to get his supper and then set up a camp before dark. John kept to himself the rest of the trip, concentrating on the road and marking up his maps with road condition information.

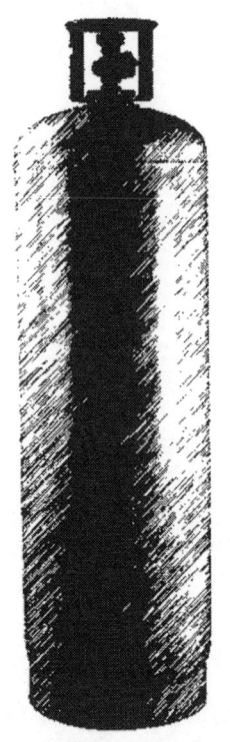

100 lb Propane Tank

The damage wasn't limited to just overpasses and bridges down; the pavement itself was badly damaged in places. The areas where the roads were displaced horizontally weren't too difficult to deal with. The vertical displacement was another thing. Sometimes there was a drop or a rise of as much as five feet or more in places. Most of the time it wasn't a problem for the four-wheel-drive truck to get around them, but that wasn't always the case.

There was less damage southwest of Springfield, but there was damage. John spent two days in the Quadraplex basement on the outskirts of Tulsa so he could meet with Colonel Andrews and his aides, filling them in on what he'd found during his trip.

When John finally got back to the Farm early fall, he saw where repairs had been made on some of the buildings, especially the greenhouses. John immediately pitched in to help with the repairs, and then the harvesting. John listened to the Amateur and shortwave bands nearly every evening.

The New Madrid earthquakes were continuing, just as they had in 1811 and 1812. Some as large, or larger than the first few. Reports were coming in from all over the Mississippi River drainage area. Places that had survived all the war and the weather could throw at them were essentially destroyed by the earthquakes. The New Orleans, Mobile, and Houston areas subsided and the Gulf rushed in. Only high rise islands remained of the cities.

The winter wasn't quite as early as the previous winter, but it was just as bad. The Farm was isolated for December and January due to the massive snowfalls. When the Farm dug out the following spring, the residents found that a good fourth of their market had disappeared or died off during the winter.

The military, at least in Tulsa, was disbanded and individual service people were left to their own devices. John talked to Colonel Andrews before he headed for his home in Missouri. "I don't know what has happened," the Colonel said. "We lost communication with what Federal Administration there was. I don't know if they were destroyed, gave up, or what. The last orders I got were to disband my command and return to private life."

"Your family will be glad to see you, Colonel."

"I'm sure they will. But I don't like leaving things hanging. Most of my people are good people. We were told to issue each person in our command a firearm, that didn't already have one, and give everyone five-hundred rounds of ammunition for it, along with a hundred one-ounce silver rounds and ten one-ounce gold coins. I am afraid there is an element that may try to take advantage of the locals and set up a power base."

"We'll be on our guard," John said.

A small smile crossed the Colonel's face. "I believe you will be able to handle it, if it occurs. Now, the other equipment will be disabled and the parts cached, but left otherwise intact, for possible future use. That includes caching ammunition.

"Being the distrusting sort that I am, I was able to acquire additional ammunition over and above the revised TOE (Table of equipment) for my command. There will be some small arms ammunition left over and above what I'm supposed to have, after distributing what I'm supposed to. If a couple of trucks were to show up before the ammunition is cached, one might be able to acquire a few hundred cases of small arms ammo."

"I will keep it in mind," John said, also with a small smile.

"Another point. The caches we do make need to be in safe places. Don't want just anyone digging them up and taking off in an Abrams Tank."

"It just so happens I know a few caching spots where I don't think you would have to worry about such things happening."

"I thought you might."

A larger smile appeared on John's face as he said, "Actually, if it was within regulations, I think I could probably contract the entire operation for you."

Colonel Andrews looked startled for a moment, and then he too grinned. "The government has been known to use contractors. I think we can work something out. Would silver and gold be all right for payment?"

"Absolutely. Where'd you get the gold and silver?"

"We received it just before we got orders to disband. The way I understand it, they started up one of the mints and produced a bunch of silver and gold coins using the old dies, to help commerce. We were supposed to start paying the troops a little, and start paying for what we'd been giving scrip."

"But not pay off the scrip?" John asked.

Colonel Andrews shook his head. The two men shook hands. Colonel Andrews gave John several names of people in his command that might be willing to help with the caching and mothballing work. As soon as the meeting with Colonel Andrews was over, John went looking for the people.

It took a while, but when John went to the quad basement for the evening he had a work force of seven soon to be ex-military people that would move the military equipment to the Farm and disable and mothball it. Those that wanted to stay at the Farm would be allowed to. Those that didn't would get a tank of fuel for a vehicle if they had one, and a week's food. If they didn't have a vehicle, they would get a month of travel food.

He and Adam would do the actual caching of the critical parts. The process was done by July 1st. Most of the rest of the military detachment was long gone. Colonel Andrews went out to the Farm to fill the fuel wagon he was towing behind the cargo trailer that the Humvee he'd been allocated was pulling.

When he offered to pay, Adam, after seeing a small shake of the head by John, declined. "You've done your best to try to normalize the area. We thank you for that. You have our frequencies. Stay in contact, if you will."

The Colonel hesitated for a long time, and then went to bed of the pickup style Humvee. "You guys take this. I'm not comfortable hanging on to it. It's not legally mine and I feel bad about how much we got from you guys, with only the scrip in return.

There was a wooden case in the back of the Humvee much like the ammunition crates they'd moved from Tulsa. Colonel Andrews opened it slightly. It was three-quarters full of neatly rolled gold and silver coins. "Consider it payment for the scrip."

Colonel Andrews shook hands with the two men, climbed into the Humvee and headed home to Missouri to be with his family.

The Colonel had known the people in his command well. Less than a month after the military had disbanded, a group that had come together, with a few of the local element, attacked the Farm with the intention of getting the military hardware for their own use. To set up the power base that the Colonel had mentioned.

But the Farm was well defended, with everyone of age both capable and willing to lend a hand to repel an attack. Of the twenty-seven people in the attacking force, three lived long enough to talk to John and Adam.

"We thought you were just a bunch of farmers…" was the last thing one of them said before dying of his wounds. The other two were tried and hanged two weeks later. They were the last of the trouble makers for a long time to come.

The Farm was prepared for the long haul. One hundred and three years later when the first national elections were held, the Farm had a nominee for not only Congress, but the presidency as well.

The End

THANK YOU FOR READING

Jerry D. Young's

Survival Fiction Library

Book Two: Low Profile

LIKE THIS BOOK?

See more great books at www.creativetexts.com

"SIMPLER TIMES"
"BUGGING HOME"
"THE SLOW ROAD"
"PLANNING PAYS OFF"
"RUDY'S PREPAREDNESS SHOP"
"CME: CORONAL MASS EJECTION"
"HOME SWEET BUNKER"
"THE HERMIT"

& MANY MORE GREAT
POST-APOCALYPTIC FICTION
& OTHER TITLES

THANK YOU!

MEET THE AUTHOR

Jerry D Young was born at home, in Senath, Missouri July 3, 1953. At age 5 the family rented a small farm house on an active farm 40 miles southwest of St. Louis. While the family weren't farmers, they lived something of a homestead type life, raising a milk cow, sometimes two, and calves, a pig or two, chickens, and the occasional goat. Along with the stock, a large garden helped to feed Jerry's three brothers and two sisters for several years. Fishing and hunting contributed to the pantry, as did foraging the wild edibles on the property.

At the age of 14, the family, minus a brother and two sisters that were now adults and on their own, moved back to Senath. Having been encouraged from an early age to read, Jerry was a regular patron of the Senath Branch Library. A love of a good story was born within him, and shortly before graduating high school, for a lack of stories that he liked at the library, he began to write short vignettes, and started taking notes for stories that he wanted to tell. Jerry eventually began to write in earnest and now has more than 100 titles to his credit including Prep/PAW stories, Action/Adventure, and a few of the romance type stories that first got him started.

Made in the USA
Lexington, KY
05 April 2018